STORIES OF THE *Rich*
OF THE
AND
Famous

AIKEN'S WINTER COLONY
IN THE GILDED AGE

David M. Tavernier

outskirtspress
DENVER, COLORADO

Stories of the Rich and Famous
Aiken's Winter Colony in the Gilded Age

Cover Photo - Mrs. Hitchcock prepares to lead student riders on the Aiken drag hunt. The Aiken County Historical Museum © 2012 All rights reserved - used with permission.

Outskirts Press, Inc.
http://www.outskirtspress.com

ISBN: 978-1-4327-9760-7

Outskirts Press and the "OP" logo are trademarks belonging to Outskirts Press, Inc.

PRINTED IN THE UNITED STATES OF AMERICA

To the two most important women in my life, my mother, Theresa Maynard Tavernier, who, since I was a child, always encouraged me to do my best in every endeavor, and my wife, Patrice Durban Tavernier, who has always kept me on an even keel with her valuable advice and affably loving manner.

David M. Tavernier
Aiken, S. Carolina

PREFACE

What was so special about Aiken, South Carolina, that drew the country's wealthiest and most powerful families there each winter, beginning in the late nineteenth century and continuing past World War II?

Having been born and raised in Rhode Island, I was, of course, familiar with the Vanderbilt family's Marble House and The Breakers, in Newport. As a boy I toured those mansions-turned-museums, and while impressed and fascinated with their pomp and grandiosity, I never gave another thought about the lives and times of the people who built them until I met my wife, a native of Aiken, and became a permanent resident there. Consequently, I ran head-on into a local history entwined with the activities of the country's wealthiest and most powerful people.

Upon moving to Aiken, I immediately noticed things that one would not typically find in a small southern town: mansions, polo, the mounted fox chase, the thoroughbred stables, training tracks, and a number of annual, traditional events of English origin that are associated with the gentlemanly art of fox hunting and horse racing, in addition to golf and croquet.

Initially, the question in my mind was: Out of the hundreds of small southern towns whose existence revolved around crops and cotton production, why was Aiken so different? Yes, Aiken had and still has agriculture, but its most striking characteristics, unlike other small southern towns, are the physical remains and continuing traditions that were introduced by individuals of Anglo heredity, with prodigious financial resources. What I was to learn was fascinating.

What began with the arrival of a New Orleans aristocratic family with strong northeastern societal ties in the 1880s soon became a stream that grew into a seasonal flood of winter visitors with names such as Hitchcock, Vanderbilt, Whitney, Astor, McLean, and Harriman— iconic names associated with the railroad, banking, newspaper, and insurance industries. From the highest levels of government came Roosevelt, Churchill, Bohlen, and Longworth, among others. Musical giants named Zimbalist, Casals, Stokowski, and Hofmann came. Entertainers came, such as Fred Astaire, Bing Crosby, Andy Williams, Paul Newman, and Erica Von Stade. Some bought, many built, and others leased homes they called "cottages," but could more accurately be described as mansions. Collectively they became known to native Aikenites as the "Winter Colony."

As a result of this perennial migration, it was not long after the turn of the century that this small, relatively obscure southern town became known as the "Newport of the South." It acquired other titles as well, including "Queen of Winter Resorts and "Polo Capitol of America." While most of the country at large did not know of Aiken's existence, references to it could be frequently found in the *New York Times* society column, beginning in the fall and continuing until spring each year, as social columnists tracked the migratory activities of late nineteenth and early twentieth century America's rich and famous.

Many of Aiken's winter visitors were wealthy New Yorkers who knew, intermarried, and in many cases socialized with one another. A number of them maintained chateau-like homes in the city and in wealthy, exclusive enclaves like Old Westbury and other parts of Long Island. Some were business allies, some competitors, but in many cases they shared common avocations, such as polo, golf, and thoroughbred horse racing and breeding. They hobnobbed with one another at the New York Yacht Club and Saratoga Springs, and socialized at gatherings of the Four Hundred and at exclusive New York City clubs. They were always under the watchful eyes of society columnists and others who trade on inside information.

However, in Aiken they could escape the societal microscopic scrutiny, let their hair down, and continue to enjoy their outdoor, primarily equine activities, which were suspended by cold New York winters. Their prodigious financial resources allowed them to transport their horses, their domestic staffs, families, and hangers-on via commercial and private railroad cars every November, and return in the Easter season once the northern snows were gone.

When Aiken's infrastructure to accommodate their hobbies was absent, they created them. In 1892, golf was introduced to the southeast with the construction of the now legendary Palmetto Golf Club, the first four holes built by William C. Whitney and Thomas Hitchcock of New York. Whitney Field, still in use today, was purchased by William C. Whitney in 1892, whereupon he increased its utility from simply polo to thoroughbred racing by designing and encircling it with a racing track. And they were civic-minded as well, playing leading roles in improving Aiken's quality of life. In 1917, winter colonists William Vanderbilt, Col. Anthony R. Kuser, and Mrs. C. Oliver Iselin, of America's Cup fame, led the effort in providing most of the funding for Aiken's first hospital. What today is known as Hitchcock Woods was a forest preserve bought by the Hitchcock and Whitney families and maintained for riding and fox hunting, and whose bridle trails, created by the original owners, are still in use today.

The Aiken Preparatory School, dedicated to providing a classical education to upcoming young gentlemen, was founded in 1916 by winter colonist Louise Hitchcock, and in 1919, her cousin, Marie Hofmann founded the Fermata School for Girls. They were responsible for bringing cultural performances to the Aiken Opera House each season. Without the winter colonists, Pablo Casals, Josef Hofmann, Leopold Stokowski, Caruso, and Will Rogers would never have found their way to this small southern town. While their reasons for bringing musical giants to Aiken were self-serving, these performances were open to local townspeople who welcomed these otherwise locally unattainable events.

Where wealth was to travel and congregate, one could always expect that politicians would soon follow, and Aiken was no exception. FDR was an occasional visitor, as well as 1920s U.S. Speaker of the House, Nicholas Longworth, who was to die in Aiken during what was rumored as a tryst with a wealthy socialite. Winston Churchill was a guest at the Willcox Inn, and at least one New York senator owned a cottage on Hayne Avenue, close to downtown.

Researching Aiken's history was made easier due to the abundance of information available. Aiken is populated by residents who are fiercely proud of their heritage and home, many of whom have passed down oral histories through the generations, and a number of them have left written documentation. The lives and activities of the rich and famous who came to Aiken each year are well documented by a number of sources, as many of these individuals have left their imprints on the country's business, political, and societal histories. The *Aiken Standard* newspaper and *The New York Times* archives possess a wealth of information on the winter colonists and their activities in Aiken and New York. Additionally, numerous books have been written about the lives of many of these people, and those are readily available.

The people and places in these stories are real, and while many of the events described actually took place, some are of my own imagination, and as such, this work falls in the category of historical fiction. Where I have used my own invention, I did so to effectively convey an event and, in a few cases, to pique the reader's interest.

TABLE OF CONTENTS

AIKEN'S BEGINNING AND THE FOUNDING OF THE WINTER COLONY

Historians can trace the discovery of the general area of what is now largely Aiken County back to the Spanish conquistador DeSoto. His exploration of the Savannah River in 1540 and his encounter with Native Americans at the village of Cofitachiqui[1] exceed the scope of this brief history, whose purpose is to acquaint the reader with the circumstances and events that led to the creation of the city of Aiken, and why it was so attractive to so many people before the War Between the States and after, an attraction that continues to this day.

The major factors that contributed to Aiken's founding and early success were: 1) The migration of lowcountry planters escaping summertime heat, which brought disease, particularly malaria and yellow fever, to marshy plantation areas resulted in Aiken's growing reputation as a health resort; 2) The textile manufacturing and kaolin mining industries; 3) The development of the railroad.

These factors brought about developing conditions that set the stage for Aiken's post War Between the States discovery by northern industrialists, sportsmen, millionaires, politicians, and high society families seeking a healthy climate and mild winters, where they could avoid the harsh winter climate of the northeast and Midwest. Aiken's antebellum-rooted reputation for being a place for healthy living started the momentum that would grow following the war, now appealing to a very different clientele. Had it not been for the lowcountry planters establishing Aiken as a healthful retreat, one can only speculate on

---

[1] The tribal village Cofitachiqui was renamed Silver Bluff in Beech Island. It was given that name by an Irishman, George Galphin, who established a trading post there around 1735.

the timing or even if the winter colony would have ever developed to the extent it did in Aiken.

MIGRATION OF THE LOWCOUNTRY PLANTERS

Geographically, the lowcountry follows an area of coastal region along the Santee, Cooper, and Ashley rivers of South Carolina. The term "planters" denotes not only those engaged in farming but also a "planter class." The planter class also included professional men such as lawyers, doctors, clergymen, educators, and writers, some who were planters themselves or were related to planter families. In many cases the non-planters of that class would have shared cultural values, family ties, and a common ancestry with farmer planters. These are the individuals who, primarily after 1790, would leave the lowcountry area in late spring and would head for either the "sea" on the eastern South Carolina coast or the "pine" in the northern and western inland areas, to escape the mosquito-borne malarial plague, which intensified with the growing summer heat.

It is theorized that summer migrations that began after 1790 were a consequence of the start of rice planting in the lowcountry. Rice, by virtue of the manner in which it is grown, necessitates a moist environment—the very same environment that nurtures mosquito populations, including the Anopheles mosquito, the bearer of malaria. Prior to that time, in the 1735 time frame, there were a small number of affluent lowcountry planters migrating to areas outside South Carolina, specifically Newport, Rhode Island, during the summer months. Most, however, prior to 1790, remained on their farms year round.

When planters did leave their farms each summer, the properties were given into the custody of hired foremen and slaves who were charged with tending the crops, operating, and protecting those properties. For many planters, packing and leaving the farm was an arduous affair involving the moving of furniture, family, relatives, and their personal effects in such volume to accommodate an extended absence. There were varied time preferences for escaping the "sickly season," as it was called. May and June were popular times for leaving, and the return was usually timed with the first or "cleansing" (hard) frost, usually coming in the November time frame.

HEADING TO THE COAST

The first groups to leave the lowcountry areas sought out the coastal beach islands, such as Sullivan's Island, and the coastal cities, primarily Charleston, Beaufort, Georgetown, and Edingsville Beach on Edisto Island. A number of families continued to visit Newport, Rhode Island. It was believed that the continuous ocean breezes would offset any swamp vapors, and the salt air would deter the production of mosquitoes. In actuality this was, to a certain extent, correct, despite their limited knowledge of malaria, its proliferation, and treatment. Charleston was the first choice for many planters who bought or built townhomes there, and the city's population expanded significantly during the summer, taxing the city's water, sewage, and trash disposal resources. Whether completely factual or not, this situation took most of the blame for the rise of yellow fever there. Consequently, many left for nearby Sullivan's Island, where fresh ocean air was believed to be the panacea to summer's health perils.

These well-heeled, summertime refugees were always in search of new locales that were convenient and offered a dry, breezy, mosquito-free environment.

HEADING INLAND

In the later antebellum years and in connection with the development of the Charleston to Hamburg[2] railroad line, it was discovered

---

2   Hamburg, founded in 1821, was located across from Augusta, Georgia, on the South Carolina side of the Savannah River and served as a consolidation point for cotton shipments to the coast. Hamburg is no longer extant.

that Aiken,[3] located 120 miles northwest of Charleston, possessed all the summer environmental qualities sought by lowcountry planters. At an elevation of 510 feet above sea level, it has dry atmosphere and is consequently mosquito-free, and is heavily forested with pines that infuse the breeze with a fresh pine scent. Aiken's reputation immediately grew as a health resort along with the growing reputation of its Coker Spring, which always provided fresh, cold water. By 1833, two years before the City was granted a charter, Charleston newspapers were publicizing Aiken's healthy environment and its increasingly famous Coker Spring.

One individual who was attracted to Aiken was a Columbia, and later Charleston, businessman who was first engaged as a watchmaker, silversmith, and jeweler. He spent some time living in Edgefield, South Carolina, during a period of ill health, and became acquainted with the Aiken area. His name was William Gregg, and in 1846 he was to have a large impact on the population and economic growth of Aiken.

Aiken was not the only inland resort discovered by the lowcountry migrants. Summerville was convenient to Charleston area planters; Walterboro appealed to Ashepoo and Combahee river planters; and Adam's Run and Whiteville attracted a number of Cooper River planters. Others included Pendleton, Greenville, Spartanburg, and Winnsboro. These, like Aiken, were called sandhill resorts.

THE TEXTILE INDUSTRY IN AIKEN

In December of 1845, a charter was granted to William Gregg by the legislature for the establishment of the Graniteville Company, a textile concern. The mill, which was completed in 1846, was located in Horse Creek Valley. Gregg was the fourth largest shareholder in the company, whose stock was held by a number of Charleston investors. Since Gregg had most of the ideas and had spent time in New England

---

3   Aiken was founded in 1835 and named after William Aiken, president of the South Carolina Railroad and Canal Company.

to learn the textile industry, he was made president of the company. It seemed to Gregg that if cotton was being grown here, then its conversion into cloth should be here, rather than transporting it raw to the North for refinement.

By the time of the company's founding, the Charleston to Hamburg railroad line had been in operation for about twelve years, and travelers and cargo were routinely coming and going the 136-mile distance between the two areas. In 1846, Gregg built a summer home on Kalmia Village in Aiken on the 5,000 acres that he acquired there, and by 1854, he all but abandoned Charleston, and Kalmia became his permanent home. Kalmia Village soon became a summer resort, as it was reported that Gregg gave fifty-five-acre tracts to several of his friends who built summer homes there.

The Graniteville Company saw slow progress during the depression of the 1850s, and indeed, Gregg lent up to $90,000 of his own money to enable its continued operation. However, during the War Between the States, the company held Confederate government contracts as a supplier of cloth and military uniforms, which allowed it to prosper. In addition to its continuously growing cotton product lines, it continued to be a supplier of military uniforms for every war thereafter. The town of Graniteville formed around the company mill and grew up in the area about three miles from Vaucluse in Aiken County. Churches, schools, homes were built, and the economy prospered in the Graniteville area as a result of Gregg's Graniteville Company.

Gregg's Graniteville Company was a major economic factor in the growth of Aiken. It provided a ready market for cotton growers, offered industrial jobs and attracted workers, and even contributed to Aiken's continued growing reputation as a winter resort among Charlestonians who either personally knew Gregg or knew of his Kalmia area landholdings that were given or sold to other migrating planter-class individuals and families.

In addition to the Graniteville Company, kaolin mining began in the mid 1800s. Kaolin is white-colored clay used in pottery production in addition to other porcelain-like products. A factory that ultimately became Southern Porcelain Manufacturing Company was established, further growing the area's economy.

Facilitating and quickening the pace of Aiken's growth was the advent of the first and longest railroad line in the country—the Charleston to Hamburg Rail Line.

THE COMING OF THE RAILROAD

In 1821, the settlement of Hamburg was founded on the South Carolina bank of the Savannah River. It was founded by George Schultz in conjunction with a cotton warehouse that he owned there, which was used for the consolidation of shipments transported by steamboats to the ever growing port of Savannah, Georgia. The city of Charleston, South Carolina, had begun to lose its dominance as a receiving port for cotton shipments and other crop goods, and by 1824, much of the trade had shifted to Savannah. Charleston was facing economic disaster.

Two Charleston businessmen, William Aiken and Alexander Black, who were familiar with some innovative English experiments using iron rails on which cars were drawn, replacing horse and wagons for transporting goods, discussed the feasibility of trying to implement the technology here to save Charleston's economic future.

Aiken, who had been friends with George Schultz, contacted him with the farsighted possibility of constructing a railed road from Charleston to Hamburg for the purpose of moving cotton and other products by rail, thereby challenging the economic dominance of Savannah's steamboats.

In 1828, a charter was granted, entitled the South Carolina Canal and Rail Road Company. The charter allowed for it to hold multiple entities, including the Charleston and Hamburg Railroad, which had been organized the previous year. It allowed for the transport of passengers as well as freight. Surveys were immediately begun at the direction of William Aiken, who was now president of the Charleston and Hamburg Railroad, and actual construction began outside[4] the city of Charleston in 1830.

Great effort was needed to overcome numerous challenges involving first-generation locomotives and engineering obstacles related to grading, bridging swamps for the laying of rails, and particularly difficult problems associated with an elevated grade as they approached the crossroads that would later be named Aiken. The question became, why worry about dealing with a significantly elevated grade creating engineering problems, when a more direct route to Hamburg on a relatively level grade could be accomplished by running rail through the area of what is now the Savannah River Site? The answer remained with a young Harvard graduate hired by William Aiken to survey the area.

Early in 1830, Aiken hired young Harvard graduate Alfred Andrew Dexter, who along with his assistant, C.O. Pascalis, were charged with surveying the route to Hamburg. They had decided on a path that would not have come through the area to become Aiken; however, in the course of Dexter's duties, he met Sara Williams, daughter of landowner William White Williams[5]. Williams had bought his large landholding from the Indians where he established his cotton plantation, whose product had to be hauled overland to Hamburg for shipment down the Savannah River. A nearby railroad would obviate the problem of transporting his crops overland, and so, when Dexter, who had fallen in love with Sara, asked for her hand, it is reported that Williams would only agree to the marriage if the railroad were routed near to his property. To this end Williams dedicated a large block of land for the laying of track at no cost to the railroad. In the end love (and

---

4   Charleston's city fathers initially prohibited the company from constructing its railed road within the city limits as a safety measure.
5   The W. W. Williams home, built in 1820, still stands at the area of South Boundary and Whiskey roads.

good business sense), won out,[6] and Dexter revised his survey route to pass within 100 yards of Williams' cotton fields and follow a line that would eventually be called Railroad Street, and later, Park Avenue in downtown Aiken. However, the challenge of negotiating a steep grade coming into town would need to be overcome. This was accomplished by installing incline planes and a winch. Near where Highland Park Avenue and Highland Park Terrace are today, there was a stationary winch that would haul cars up a steep incline plane to the depot by cable, then continue on to where it would proceed down a gravity-fed incline plane, descending through what is today the Aiken Golf Club[7] to Sand River, and thence follow a creek along a level plane to Hamburg. Other early property owners of the area who made land available to the railroad were Beverly M. Rodgers and William Moseley.

In October of 1833, the first locomotive arrived in the small settlement that in two years' time would be called Aiken. Having died in a carriage accident in 1831, William Aiken would never see his railroad enter the community that would be named in his honor in 1835.

Aiken began to flourish and prosper at a steady pace in the antebellum years as its reputation as a refuge for invalids and those seeking a milder, dry climate spread throughout the south. By 1842, Aiken's population had grown to 1,000. Products and passengers were now traveling between Charleston and Aiken in an incredible twelve hours, a tremendous innovation for that time.

Since 1820, William Mosely had operated the first general store and bank, located where the Aiken Hotel is today on the northeast corner of Laurens Street and Richland Avenue. He had been a prominent financier for loggers and other business endeavors related to product shipment down the Savannah River. The area's first church, First

---

6 Dexter and Sara Williams were married on January 7, 1834.
7 In 1853, the tracks were relocated into a cut that was hand dug running parallel to and south of Park Avenue. This was done to remove the steep grade that affected train performance and necessitated winches and cables for raising and lowering trains upon entering and leaving Aiken's train depot. This cut still exists today.

Baptist Church, was chartered in 1805 under the name Levels Baptist Church, and held services in a home where the Palmetto Golf Club is today. As the visitor population expanded, enough money was raised to build an Episcopal Church, and St. Thaddeus was constructed in 1842, largely through the sponsorship of William Aiken's widow. St. John's Methodist followed in 1857 on the corner or Richland Avenue and Newberry Street, and First Presbyterian in 1859 on the corner of Laurens Street and Park Avenue.

Built around 1850 on the southeast corner of York Street and Colleton Avenue, the York House offered thirty rooms to seasonal visitors. Around 1860, the Palmetto Inn was built on the corner of Hayne Avenue and Florence Street to accommodate seasonal visitors, an early predecessor to those that would follow as Aiken's popularity as a health resort grew.

The War Between the States left Aiken relatively unscathed, in good measure due to Confederate General Joseph Wheeler, whose 4,500 Confederate troops met Union Major General Hugh Judson Kilpatrick's 2,000 troops near today's downtown. Wheeler's troops were encamped in the area of the Williams' home on Railroad Avenue[8]. Kilpatrick's army was located near The Vale of Montmorenci[9] from whence he marched toward the Union Street area, where the train depot was located. Kilpatrick's orders from General William Sherman were to burn towns and strategic facilities as they were encountered as much as possible, including disabling railroad tracks, then join the army's main force continuing on to Columbia, and from there, continue their march to the sea. Aiken was not burned as Union forces retreated in what ended in a stalemate battle in February 1865. However, railroad transportation was disrupted when the Union army destroyed

---

8   Today it is called Park Avenue
9   A 1,000-acre plantation owned and named by Frenchman James Achille de Caradeuc in 1840. He was a construction engineer for the Charleston to Hamburg railroad, remained in Aiken, and named his plantation after the duchy in France from whence he came, Montmorenci. The Vale is extant and located on today's Old Dibble Rd.

track between Blackville and Aiken as they passed through.

Following the War Between the States and having achieved success by its growing reputation with southern planters, Aiken's marketing effort was now focused on the North. From that time forward the town's traditional clientele was altered, and now included wealthy northern winter visitors (many planters were ruined due to the ravages of the war). What was to come would totally change the town's profile and set the tone for a very different future.

POST-WAR AIKEN

Immediately following the war and with an expanding railroad network connecting Aiken with rail traffic from the north, the potential for increased growth multiplied. The town's accommodations, as evidenced by the construction of several new hotels, was testament to Aiken's growing reputation as a health resort. In 1869, the Highland Park Hotel was built as Aiken's first and largest grand tourist hotel by a group of investors from Connecticut, headed by B.P. Chatfield. It consisted of four stories sitting on twenty-three acres on Highland Park Drive. Chatfield was convinced that Aiken would continue to grow as a health resort for northerners seeking a milder climate during the winter months, and for that reason the hotel was only open from November to April. The two-story Park Avenue Hotel was built in the early 1870s across the street from the railway station to accommodate wintering northerners; then came the Willcox Hotel in 1898, and later came the Park in the Pines Hotel, and the Commercial Hotel. As the number of winter visitors grew, so did Aiken's economy. Banks, grocery stores, specialty shops, and other new businesses opened, offering resident and visitor alike more conveniences and a higher quality of life. Aiken was escaping the singular agricultural/cotton plantation definition held by most other cities in rural South Carolina as its economic diversity grew.

However, the arrival of one lady, Ms. Celestine Eustis, and her young niece, Louise Eustis of New Orleans and France in the mid 1870s, and the migration she nearly single-handedly initiated, was to begin a steady stream of new winter guests coming from the highest levels of American society. The bankers, the industrialists, the statesmen, the sportsmen, the millionaires, they came in their private railcars from the north, seeking not to escape summer plague, but harsh northern winters, and pass the season engaged in polo, golf, horse racing, hunting, and tennis, while enjoying high tea, evening soirees, musicales, elaborate dinners, and the company of fellow denizens of high society. They built magnificent homes they called "cottages"[10] and founded facilities for polo, golf, tennis, hunting, and horse racing. They established a number of Aiken traditions that continue to this day. The family names associated with this invasion were drawn from the ranks of the most powerful, wealthy, and high-born members of American society. Astors, Vanderbilts, Whitneys, Hitchcocks, Rutherfurd, Iselin, and others flocked to Aiken each November and left with the coming of spring. They came from some of the most prestigious neighborhoods in America, such as Old Westbury, Long Island; Bar Harbor, Maine; Washington DC; Manhattan, and Beacon Hill. Aiken became a resort phenomenon known to society editors of major U.S. newspapers, including the *New York Times*, and the *Washington Post*, who followed their society subjects' activities in this otherwise anonymous southern city. They gave it such descriptive names as "Newport of the South" and "Winter Playground of the Rich," among others. The name "Aiken" was even used as a communication code word by at least one U.S. emissary[11] to a foreign country who had winter ties to the city.

FOUNDING THE AIKEN WINTER COLONY

10   A home needed a minimum of twenty rooms to be classified as a "cottage." Many, such as Joye Cottage owned by millionaire William C. Whitney, had fifty rooms. Joye Cottage is extant today.

11   Willard Straight, U.S. Diplomatic Corps in Korea and China following the Boxer Rebellion

Although Celestine Eustis called New Orleans home, she was born in Paris. Celestine's father, George Eustis, was a Louisiana lawyer who became Chief Justice of the Louisiana Supreme Court. He was a founder of Tulane University and had substantial involvement in the Pontchartrain Railroad Company. Her mother, Clarisse Allain Eustis, came from a prominent French-speaking New Orleans family who enjoyed aristocratic status in their city and state. Celestine's brother, George Eustis Jr., a Louisiana lawyer and congressman, was married to Louise Morris Corcoran, the only daughter of wealthy international banker William Wilson Corcoran[12]. George and Louise were the parents of Louise Mary Eustis, who, with her aunt Celestine, was destined to cast a large shadow over Aiken, along with her husband, Thomas Hitchcock Jr. of Old Westbury, New York, who was a newspaper business heir, international polo player, and horse trainer.

In addition to being a congressman, George Eustis Jr. was appointed minister to France for the Confederate States in the 1860s. The family remained there following the War Between the States at their villa[13] in Cannes. By 1872, the five-year-old Louise had lost her parents to consumption (tuberculosis). Her spinster aunt, Celestine, and her maternal grandfather, W.W. Corcoran,[14] became her guardians.

Celestine knew about Aiken's reputation as a health resort, and she began taking her niece, who had experienced breathing problems, there in the 1870s. Louise was about ten years of age when she first came to Aiken with her aunt, an event that was to be repeated each winter with the two of them becoming increasingly attached to their new southern hometown.

Conscious of her social class, Celestine ensured that Louise spent the necessary time during her formative years with grandfather Corcoran

---

12   Corcoran founded the famous Corcoran Galleries in Washington, DC in 1854.
13   Their villa was named "Louisiana."
14   By 1857, Corcoran had already become wealthy through his banking interest. He was a founder of Riggs Bank, now known as PNC, and established the famous Corcoran Gallery in Washington DC before the outbreak of the war.

in Washington, where she was introduced to Washington and New York society. In August 1891, Louise married Thomas Hitchcock Jr. The wedding took place at Aunt Celestine's summer home, Cross Road Cottage, at Beverly Farms, Massachusetts.

By the time of Louise's marriage, Celestine had already purchased her Aiken home and several other Aiken properties as well. Initially, Louise's new husband was reluctant to spend time in a small southern town when their travel time could be better spent visiting England, where he was more comfortable and known to the equine community. However, after once visiting Aiken, Thomas found the area to be the perfect place to exercise his passion for raising and training thorough-breds. He found that Aiken's clay/sandy soil was perfect for equine traction with no adverse effect on hooves. He found that the climate (as others had already found) was most agreeable, particularly in the late fall, winter, and early spring months, for both equestrian and other outdoor activities. And with the railroad solidly in place, it would be relatively easy to transport the horses from his Old Westbury stables to Aiken each winter and extend the season for equine activities from part time to year round.

With Thomas and Louise Hitchcock and Aunt Celestine lead-ing the charge, the word rapidly spread among northern high society equestrian and hunting enthusiasts about the agreeable little city in South Carolina called Aiken, and thus began an ever growing annual migration of the richest, most powerful individuals and families in the country, which forever changed Aiken from a small health resort to a winter playground for America's elites. The following stories are about who these people were, what they did, and how their activities shaped the future of the city of Aiken, South Carolina.

IN REMEMBRANCE OF
MRS. HITCHCOCK

For the many times that I've attended St. Mary's Catholic Church in Aiken, I will never forget the morning of April 2, 1934, when funeral services were held for Mrs. Thomas Louise "Loulie"[15] Hitchcock. The church was at bursting capacity as mourners filled every pew and space; others who didn't arrive early enough were standing in the aisles and foyer, and still others were spilling out onto the front steps and the street. Every strata of Aiken society was present: locals, winter residents, and a special section designated "Colored" for the many black residents who were touched by the charitable heart of Mrs. Hitchcock. I stood proudly by my father in my Clemson College cadet uniform. As a first-year Clemson cadet, it was very unusual to be excused from school, particularly so close to finals, and it was only through my father's passionate intercession that I was allowed to be present that morning at St. Mary's, to say good-bye to a gracious lady who not only touched the heart of the community, but also left a lifetime impression on me.

I listened as the organist played a mellow dirge, and altar boys lit the funerary candles. We patiently waited for Father George Dietz to appear and begin the service. My mind began to wander and drift back to the recent past when I was a student at the Aiken Institute. The Aiken Institute, which was founded in 1891, was a private school for all students through grade twelve. The tuition was a very modest $.25 per month for in-town students until it became part of the South Carolina School System in 1935, after which it was free. The Institute

---

15   Author's note: Sources vary on the spelling of Mrs. Hitchcock's childhood diminutive. I have chosen the spelling "Loulie" as reported by her grandson Julian L. Peabody in his biography of her, *Gran, A Personal Recollection.*

today looks much as it did back then, and now serves as the Aiken Library, located on the corner of South Boundary and Whiskey Road. While I was a student there, I held part-time jobs, not because I needed to, but as my father, George Durban, was a serious businessman, he encouraged personal responsibility and, by example, a strong work ethic in his children. After many years as a banker, he acquired Laird & Son, Inc. in 1921, a bond, real estate, and insurance firm, from its founder, Mr. John Laird. And since that time it has operated as Durban-Laird's, Inc., and is still located at 155 Laurens Street. I say this because it was his infectious work ethic that, at least initially, motivated me to find part-time work with Hahn & Company and the Willcox Inn, which is how I came into contact with Mrs. Hitchcock and other seasonal residents of Aiken.

Hahn & Company was a grocery store founded in 1856 and was located on the southwest corner of Laurens Street and Richland Avenue, where Aiken Drug is today. Mr. Herman Hahn of Charleston and his brother Henry owned and operated the store that became one of the preferred purveyors to the winter, northern residents. Hahn's saw an opportunity in offering such items as caviar, Chinese preserves, pâté de foie gras, imported tea, and fresh vegetables among other things that the affluent winter residents were accustomed to having in their northern home cities like New York, Boston, and Washington. I still remember the mélange of smells from cheese, tobacco, fruit, leather, and the exposed, old wooden rafters that supported the roof, each time I entered the store. Hahn's didn't only sell groceries, but general merchandise and even building supplies as well. Hahn's also did a large business as a re-seller of cotton. My job was delivering orders to customers, including Mrs. Hitchcock.

In my deliveries I dealt with these customers' domestic staffs most of the time, but occasionally I had the opportunity to be a witness to the activities of some of the most wealthy and powerful people in the country. The group was made up of bankers, industrialists, politicians, philanthropists, sportsmen, and other professionals. They were collectively known to the locals as the "Winter Colony," and they came to Aiken every winter for its mild climate, which made it possible for them to enjoy outdoor activities such as polo, golf, fox hunting, and horse racing, while missing the harsh northern winters. They were a pampered group who, in addition to sports, enjoyed daily rounds of luncheons, dinners, picnics, balls, and high tea throughout the winter months.

It was Celestine Eustis, then Louise Hitchcock and her husband Thomas who were responsible for sparking interest in Aiken with their wealthy society friends from the North. The prime winter season lasted from mid November through March. Those were the busiest times at Hahn & Company.

It was in 1877 when Mrs. Hitchcock, a girl of ten and known as Louise "Loulie" Eustis, came with her aunt, Celestine Eustis, to Aiken for health reasons. Aiken had already been known to South Carolina lowcountry plantation owners as a place of refuge to escape the unhealthy swamp and insect infestations that occurred along the humid coastal areas during certain times of the year. Louise had come from Cannes, France, where she was born in 1867 following her father's service as attaché to the Confederate minister to France during the War Between the States. The family had remained in France following the war and settled at the family home, Villa Louisiana. Within five years of each other, and by March of 1872, young Loulie's parents both succumbed to consumption, and her spinster aunt, Celestine, became her guardian, along with her maternal grandfather, Mr. W.W. Corcoran, a wealthy international banker and philanthropist from Washington[16], with whom she spent a few years prior to arriving in Aiken. Louise's mother had been Mr. Corcoran's only surviving child.

As a high school student I had little interest in learning the

---

16   In 1874, Corcoran founded the Corcoran Gallery in Washington, DC.

backgrounds and history of the Winter Colony residents, but that was before I began working at Hahn's and the Willcox Inn, where so many of these fascinating individuals were customers.

In 1891, Louise Eustis was married to Mr. Thomas F. Hitchcock of Westbury, Long Island, New York. He was the son of Thomas Hitchcock, a lawyer and newspaper owner in New York. Educated in Oxford, England, he had been an avid horseman since childhood, a polo player who also took part in Steeplechase events in England and in the U.S. He introduced polo to Aiken in 1882 and played on the International Polo Team, representing America, in 1886. He became known as the Patron Saint of Polo because of his devotion to the development of young polo players in Long Island and Aiken. It was not unusual to see Mr. Hitchcock in the company of fellow polo players as they socialized on many afternoons at the Willcox.

The Willcox Hotel, as it was originally known, grew in a most unique and interesting way, from a catering business operated by Mr. Frederick Willcox and his Swedish-born, gourmet chef wife from their home on the corner of Colleton and Chesterfield. It was Louise Hitchcock who approached Mr. Frederick Willcox about building a hotel.

By 1898, Mrs. Hitchcock had begun to make her stamp on Aiken, and had already persuaded many of her society friends from the North to join her for the winter months. Many of these visitors who were not staying with friends lodged at the Highland Park Hotel, the largest, most luxurious hotel in the area until 1898, when it was destroyed by fire. The hotel occupied the area overlooking the Aiken Golf Club on what is now Highland Park Terrace and the immediate surrounding area. As I'm told, it was Mrs. Hitchcock who became concerned about accommodations for friends following the hotel fire. She already knew about the Willcox' skill in catering events as she had used their services in the past, and now she urged them to open a hotel and fill the void created by the destruction of the Highland Park.[17]

Using their original home as a base, Frederick and his wife added on until the building spread over a full block and consisted of two long wings joined by a central ballroom. When I was employed at the Inn, it was managed by Mr. Frederick's son Bert, who took over management there in 1928. By that time the Inn had a solid reputation for being an elite establishment, in the English club style, that indulged the needs and whims of its most rich and famous clientele. I remember the gay and lavish parties that took place in the ballroom, and helping to cater the picnics following the drag hunts through Hitchcock Woods. The guest list at the Willcox once included such famous names as Vanderbilt, Harriman, Pulitzer, McCormick, Iselin, Grace, and Hofmann. Visitors included John Jacob Astor, Ambassador Charles E. Bohlen, and Mrs. John Barrymore, wife of actor John Barrymore. Foreign guests included Mr. and Mrs. Winston Churchill, Princess Alexis Obolensky, and the Count and Countess Bernadotte of Sweden. There were those from industry such as Doris Duke, Horace Dodge, and P.S. Lorillard, among others.

Most of the time my work at the Willcox took place on the catering side of the business. Many times I would help with delivering and setting up the elaborate picnic lunches that were served in the woods following a drag hunt. Drag hunts took place on Tuesdays, Thursdays, and Saturdays. I usually worked the youth drag hunts on Saturdays, which always began at 11 a.m. They were composed of boys from Aiken Preparatory School, and girls from the Fermata School, and were led by several adults. Little did I know that on one certain drag hunt, I would be witness to a tragedy that would rock the society world in general, and Aiken in particular.

Prior to my employment at the Willcox, I had never seen a drag hunt or an "axe party" firsthand. Again, it was Mr. and Mrs. Hitchcock

---

17   A second Highland Park Hotel was built circa 1914 on the site of its predecessor. It also burned in the 1940s, and the remains were torn down.

and their equestrian friends who introduced these activities to Aiken. A drag hunt was a mock fox hunt where a scent would be dragged along a predetermined path through the woods. Except for Master of the Hounds, the hunt's leader, participants would not know the trail to be followed until the hounds were released and the hunt began. Jumps were set up along the trail, testing both rider and horse as they pursued the hounds to the sound of the hunting horn. "Axe parties" were joint efforts by the horsemen, horsewomen, and their friends, who would go into the woods and forge new hunting trails by chopping down trees, clearing brush, and creating new jumps. Both these events would end with a reward to the participants in the form of elegant picnics in the woods, served on porcelain plates framed by crystal and silver. These were often catered by the Willcox.

A few years following their marriage, the Hitchcocks bought a home from the LeGare family located at the end of Laurens Street. The LeGares had been a prominent Charleston family who used the property as a summer retreat. Mrs. Hitchcock named the place "Mon Repos,"[18] meaning My Resting Place. The home was adjacent to what would become Hitchcock Woods, an 8,000-acre forested area that was incrementally acquired and added to the Hitchcocks' real estate holdings. Ms. Celestine Eustis was first to begin buying portions of the area, then Mr. Hitchcock added to it, and finally, fellow horseman, New York attorney, and former Secretary of the Navy, William C. Whitney purchased additional areas.[19] The purpose was to preserve the forest and also provide a place for their equestrian activities. When Mr. Whitney died in 1904, the Hitchcock family acquired his portion of the woods. And that is where most of the equestrian activities took place, along with Whitney Field, which was used for polo and horse racing.[20] In

---

18 Mon Repos is no longer extant.

19 In 1897, William C. Whitney acquired "Joye Cottage," which is extant and occupies an entire block of Easy Street.

20 William Whitney purchased Aiken's first polo field and racetrack, and was a founder of the Palmetto Club, both in 1892. The track and woods were later held in the Whitney Trust Foundation to benefit the City of Aiken.

1939, The Hitchcock Foundation was created to accept and hold the annual, successive transfer of the family's property, area by area, with the intent that the woods benefit the residents and citizens of Aiken for generations to come.

By 1909, Mrs. Hitchcock had four children: Celestine Eustis "Titine," born 28 June 1892 in Massachusetts; Helen, born 1898 in Aiken; Thomas "Tommy" Jr., born 11 February 1900 in Aiken; and Francis "Frankie," born 17 November 1908, in Long Island, New York. Tommy, the eldest son, had been sent off to Massachusetts to be schooled, and by 1916, Louise couldn't bear the thought of parting with her youngest child, Frankie, while the family wintered in Aiken. Her solution to the problem was simple: In her usual outgoing style she founded a new school for boys, The Aiken Preparatory School. She enlisted the help of other Winter Colony residents, and was the driving force in forging a curriculum based on the English style of classical education, combined with horsemanship and dedicated to turning out young gentlemen. The student roster mirrored the elite names of the Winter Colony: Von Stade, Whitney, Knox, Mead, Mills, and Wright, among others. The school still occupies the area on Richland Avenue to Barnwell Avenue between Florence and Lancaster streets.

In the autumn of 1933, I entered Clemson College and never expected to be back working at either Hahn's or the Willcox, at least not before the summer months. It was during my first Christmas vacation from Clemson that Mr. Bert, from the Willcox, came to our home and asked if I could help with an upcoming event that they were catering in the preserve on Tuesday, December 26th. He explained that Mrs. Hitchcock would be leading the youth drag hunt that morning at eleven and that he was short of staff due to the holiday season. He was hoping that I could come in and help with the picnic. As much as I preferred to relax at home after a grueling first semester at Clemson, I reluctantly agreed to help out.

That Tuesday morning was unusually beautiful, with a warm sun creating a dappled sparkle as it knifed through the tall pines and the leafless winter hardwoods. The girls from the Fermata School and the boys from Aiken Prep were on holiday and would be taking part with the adults, along with Mrs. Hitchcock, who would be acting as M.F.H.[21] All met at the rendezvous clearing with handlers and their hounds. One of Mrs. Hitchcock's servants had earlier that morning dragged the selected trail with the scent, and no one except for her, and the now straining and anxious hounds, knew the route for today's ride.

As my Willcox colleagues and I were beginning the initial setup of tables and linens, riders continued to file into the clearing on their mounts. Dressed in their green felt-lined jackets and white breeches, they vied for position as the hunting horn called, the hounds released, and all with thumping hooves raced to see who would be first behind Mrs. Hitchcock's mare, Morning Mist.[22]

Back at the clearing we went about our business of setting up the silver service and porcelain, while others were checking that the hot food remained hot and the cold drinks cold. All of a sudden, and long before the hunt should have ended, we saw riders charging up the trail at full gallop, shouting at the top of their lungs and leading one of the many horse-drawn wagons that would usually follow the hunts as spectators. An accident had happened early in the hunt where Mrs. Hitchcock's mount failed to clear a small brush fence, tripped through its top, and caused her to fall headlong to the ground. She now lay unmoving in the wagon's bed.

Her injury appeared serious, but just how serious we were not aware until the final diagnosis determined that she had broken two vertebrae in her neck. She was now paralyzed. There was nothing the medicine of 1933 could do, and she was sent to total rest in her second-floor bedroom at Mon Repos. Miss Bye, her nurse and secretary, was there round the clock. There were good and bad days following the accident,

---

21   Master of Fox Hounds
22   Mrs. Hitchcock's beloved mount, Cavalier, was by 1927 retired from sporting due to age, and Morning Mist was a younger mare in the Mon Repos stable.

and she spent her conscious hours dictating and receiving letters from friends around the country. With the absence of her cheerful ways and boundless energy, the activities at Mon Repos were extremely quiet for this time of year. As winter morphed into spring, her strength continued to ebb until she finally slipped away in the early hours of Easter morning, April 1, 1934—a sad day, and a great loss for my hometown.

The deep basal chords of the church's organ, growing ever louder, and the sweet, soapy scent of incense awakened me from my mental wandering, as I was returned to reality and St. Mary's, where the funeral processional had begun. From the back of the church first came the Hitchcock family, whose ladies were dressed in white,[23] then came the altar boys bearing a tall crucifix, followed by Father Dietz disbursing plumes of incense as he slowly made his way up the center aisle. Next came the cherry wood coffin festooned with jasmine and azaleas, borne by six of Mrs. Hitchcock's younger male black servants. Throughout the ceremony I could hear the tearful whimper from many of the women, the clearing of throats, the occasional sighs, and the unrestrained outpouring of emotion from the section reserved for "Colored." As I first mentioned, not a space was vacant in the entire church, and indeed I could even hear the wheezed breathing from some of the mourners during the soundless pauses of Father Dietz's homily. At the conclusion of the rites, the coffin was taken by horse-drawn wagon to Mon Repos for burial. The graveside ceremony was private, attended only by family, close friends, and the household staff. Mrs. Hitchcock was laid to rest near the grave of her aunt, Celestine Eustis, adjacent to the garden that was so lovingly tended by Ms. Eustis during her life at Mon Repos.

This is as I, George Durban Jr., remember it in the ninety-second and final year of my life in Aiken. Mrs. Hitchcock was the Grand Lady of Aiken who, by her generosity, actions, and example, shaped the character and many of the lasting places and institutions that account

---

23 It was Mrs. Hitchcock's request that her family dress in white for her funeral. It is unknown if this stemmed from traditions associated with her paternal origins in New Orleans, where it is a custom, or whether she wanted the family to celebrate her life instead of observing her death.

for the high quality of life that still exists here today. We are forever in her debt.

THE REST OF THE STORY

George Durban, Jr. took his place in his father's bond, insurance, and real estate business following his graduation from Clemson College in 1937. He served in the U.S. Coast Guard during World War II, and following his father's death in the early 1950s, he continued to operate and grow the business for many years until passing it on to his son. In those early years working side by side with his father, he took on the management of a number of wealthy winter colonists' estates, such as the W.R. Grace estate, overseeing them in the off season. Mr. Durban passed away in 2007.

Thomas Hitchcock, Sr. played a prominent role in popularizing the sport of polo and became a Hall of Fame horse trainer. He was known as the Father of American Polo and promoted the sport in Long Island, New York, and in Aiken beginning in the early 1880s. He was also widely known as a breeder/trainer of champion thoroughbreds. Hitchcock died on September 29, 1941 and was buried alongside his wife Louise at their Aiken home, Mon Repos. His son, Tommy Hitchcock Jr., following in his father's footsteps, became an internationally acclaimed polo player. He also became a war hero, flying with the Lafayette Escadrille in World War I, and an Army Air Corps pilot in World War II, where he lost his life.

Louise Eustis Hitchcock was an unpretentious member of American high society. Unlike society women of her day, she was known for her horsemanship (she dared to ride astride), fox hunting (she actually took part in the hunt), and marksmanship (she could fire a rifle as well as any man), while simultaneously knowing how to be the most gracious hostess. Her selfless, humanitarian way was known throughout the community. It is reported that she had a practice of scanning the tax foreclosure listings in the newspaper and anonymously paying taxes on homes, saving many for people who hardly, if at all, knew her. In the north, her influence was such that many of the wealthy winter colonists came to Aiken initially because of their relationship with her and the esteem in which she was held.

JOSEF HOFMANN'S RECITAL

I remember meeting Mrs. Marie Eustis Hofmann in person for the first time when my father, Frederick Willcox, was absent from Aiken for several weeks. It was left to me to make the catering arrangements for another elegant soiree that she was planning at her thirty-four-room home, "Fermata,"[24] located across the bridge on Laurens Street, just a short distance from her first cousin, Louise Eustis Hitchcock's home, Mon Repos. She always dealt with my father, as he was the founder of our family business, The Willcox Inn, and I believe she had a greater comfort level dealing with a person who was part of her generation rather than a younger person. However, on this occasion arranging the details of her soiree fell to me. Of course I knew a lot about her from the society newspaper articles, and those of her famous husband, Josef Hofmann, who was the leading, internationally acclaimed pianist of the day; she had also been a good customer of ours for years.

Mrs. Hofmann's events were grand affairs, attended by her winter colony[25] friends, and always seemed to include a houseguest or two, usually someone who was preeminent in the musical world. The Aiken winter colony was continuing to expand in 1924, and now included an ever growing number of New York socialites with names that would be recognized anywhere: Vanderbilt, Whitney, Grace, and Zeigler. They came for the mild winters and the excellent equine training and racing environment. It was not uncommon to find such musical giants as world renowned cellist Pablo Casals, or violinist Efrem Zimbalist, or the celebrated European soprano, Marcella Sembrich, among the Hofmann's invited guests. They, along with others in the musical world, were colleagues and friends of Josef

---

24 The word "fermata" is a musical term meaning rest or stop. Fermata is no longer extant.
25 By the 1920s and '30s there were 100 or more winter colony homes in Aiken.

Hofmann. And the upcoming event would indeed be very special because it was being held to honor Mr. Hofmann's piano recital at the Aiken Opera House[26] on Park Avenue, January 16, 1924. The recital marked the opening of the Pro Arte Society, a musical appreciation group dedicated to serving the Aiken community, which was recently organized by Mrs. Hofmann. Her party was to take place immediately following the recital.

I remember my father telling us about Marie Eustis' family, since he had known them years before building the Willcox, back when he and my mother operated their catering business from our home kitchen on Colleton Avenue.

Marie Clarisse Eustis, first cousin to Louise Eustis Hitchcock, was born on March 22, 1866 in New Orleans. Her family were members of Louisiana's beau monde, and her father, James Biddle Eustis, had served as U.S. Senator from Louisiana and, in 1893, as the first ambassador to France appointed by President Grover Cleveland. Prior to that time the ambassadorial post there was ministerial. Marie's mother, Ellen Buckners Eustis, reigned over New Orleans society from her palatial home, where Marie learned and performed piano and dance, and attended the coming-out balls held during the Mardi Gras season. The family first came to Aiken when Marie's father experienced failing health and was urged by his spinster sister, Celestine Eustis—who had already established a home for her orphaned niece, Louise—to join them in the healthy and mild winter climate offered by the Aiken countryside. Thus, from childhood began Marie Eustis' love affair with Aiken, which continued throughout her lifetime.

Marie's marriage to Hofmann wasn't her first. She was originally married to her first cousin, George Eustis, Louise Hitchcock's brother. While this arrangement did cause some family discomfort, and a few raised eyebrows around town, everyone became accustomed to

---

26 The Aiken Opera House is no longer extant. It occupied the area on Park Avenue where the Aiken City Hall is now located.

the union, which lasted thirteen years and produced one son, George Eustis Jr.

Marie's husband was an outdoor sportsman and polo player who loved to spend his time riding through Hitchcock Woods and at Mr. Whitney's polo field. My father remembered him well, as George enjoyed socializing at the Willcox Inn with his sporting friends, loved his gin, and had a way of being quite flamboyant at times.

Events leading to Marie's second marriage were characterized by three chance meetings, separated by years, which led her to ultimately marry Josef Hofmann. Those encounters served to create a story that defies any sense of probability and, although true, is normally the mortar of romantic fiction.

When she was about twenty-one years old, she accompanied her father to a piano concert in Boston to hear the Polish child prodigy Josef Hofmann, a boy nine years of age who was billed by a contemporary publicity poster as "The Greatest Genius on the Pianoforte since the days of Mozart." Following the performance, her father suggested they go backstage to meet the young pianist. Upon meeting him, they observed an emotionless, reserved child who presented a distracted stare, not acknowledging anyone with eye contact or animation. That year Hofmann was touring the U.S., far from his native Poland, a child unaccustomed to the mannerisms and customs of Americans and who confined himself to his piano technique with little or no interaction with patrons or well-wishers. He would carry a vestige of this reserved trait throughout his life. From that time forward, with the exception of one encounter in Charleston in later years, including the entire time span of her marriage to George Eustis, and like the two strangers that they were, Marie never thought of or spoke to him, and indeed in later years Hofmann never remembered their first meeting. But, approximately eighteen years from that first meeting, as fate would have it, Hofmann was engaged to play in a musicale at the Aiken winter colony home, "Joye Cottage,"[27] owned by Harry Payne Whitney, and Marie was an invited guest along with most of the winter colony. As it is told, she arrived late and was roundly noticed as she shimmered through the door wearing a lavender silken ensemble with her dark hair coiffed high upon her head. She was thirty-eight years old and radiant. Following his performance, she and Hofmann spoke at length; she impressed by his technique and dynamic virtuosity, he impressed by her musical knowledge. He was twenty-seven years of age.

Within a short period of time of their second meeting, and in connection with her now estranged husband, George, who had taken George Jr. to a small fishing village frequented by tourists on the Baltic Sea, Marie followed along in order to be reunited with her son. After being there a week and while strolling the beach, she came across a man seated on a folding chair with a sketch board in hand, and immediately recognized him as Josef Hofmann. The gods had spoken! Fate had insisted that a permanent union be made, and against her family's protests, they planned a private wedding ceremony attended by close friends in late October 1905.

A honeymoon had to wait, but in 1906, while Josef finished his European autumn tour, they vacationed in the Baltic region, bought a Swiss chateau near Potsdam on the shore of Lake Heilegen, which she named "Beaumaroche,"[28] and on November 8th of that year, Marie gave birth there, to a daughter who was named Josefa.

For the next few years, Marie accompanied her husband on his 1907 musical performance tour of Russia, followed by Mexico and the U.S. in 1908, and back to Russia in 1909. His performances were always enthusiastically received, and the little family's fortunes were on the rise. For all of their European travel, Christmas was always spent at Fermata in Aiken. Christmas in Aiken was a concession to Marie,

---

27   Harry Payne Whitney was the son and heir of lawyer and New York streetcar czar William C. Whitney, who owned the cottage until his death in October 1904. Joye Cottage is extant and occupies an entire block on Easy Street.

28   When breaking from the concert tour in Europe, Marie would take time to relax at Beaumaroche.

as Josef made it clear that he had no interest in outdoor sports, society gossip, balls or parties.

By my third planning meeting with Mrs. Hofmann, she had begun to gain confidence in my ability to successfully handle her social gathering and even called me "Bertie." She impressed upon me that very important people from her Pro Arte Society would be in attendance, including Mme. Marcella Sembrich, Polish-born International soprano; Mme. Alma Gluck, operatic soprano and wife of acclaimed violinist Efrem Zimbalist; Mrs. Gertrude Vanderbilt Whitney, Vanderbilt heir and wife of Harry Payne Whitney; Mrs. Thomas Hastings, wife of the New York architect who designed the New York Library and Tomb of the Unknowns in Washington; Mrs. Edward Curtis Bok, *Saturday Evening Post* and *Ladies Home Journal* publishing heir, and founder of Philadelphia's Curtis Institute; Mrs. E. H. Harriman, widow of the railroad tycoon; Mrs. Thomas Hitchcock, her cousin and leading lady of the winter colony; Mrs. C. Oliver Iselin of America's Cup fame; and Mrs. Robert H. Wilds, a close friend and wife of a prominent Aiken doctor. She also had two important houseguests who would be in attendance, Mr. Pablo Casals and Mr. Leopold Stokowski, director of the Philadelphia Orchestra.[29] Mr. Stokowski had agreed to introduce Mr. Hofmann at the recital, and Mr. Casals had agreed to be soloist for Pro Arte's opening concert for the following year, 1925. Others among her invited guests included: Mr. and Mrs. Eugene Grace, Dr. and Mrs. J. L. Todd, Mr. and Mrs. J. Hopkins Smith, and Mr. and Mrs. Frederick A. Snow. They would also accompany Mrs. Hofmann in the opera house box seating that she had reserved through Mr. Welborn, Aiken Opera House manager. Others would also attend, bringing her guest list to seventy attendees, a modest-sized group by winter colony standards.

Our business always did well when catering parties for the winter

---

29   Upon emigrating to the U.S. from England in 1905, Stokowski was hired as organist and choir director of St. Bartholomew's Church in New York, where the Vanderbilts and other Aiken winter colonists were congregants. He began conducting the Cincinnati Orchestra in 1909, then the Philadelphia in 1912.

colony residents, partially because they always demanded the best French wines, champagne, and Canadian and Scotch whiskeys, fully ignoring prohibition, which was in force at that time. It took my father some years and risk to develop reliable supply channels for these "refreshments," but offering them made our business flourish and generated handsome profits.

Mrs. Hofmann's social gathering would feature French champagne, Bordeaux wines, and selected choice hors d'oeuvre: escargot in shell; Brie en croute; assorted finger sandwiches; Louisiana crawfish boudin; stuffed grape leaves; duck liver, forest mushroom, and French truffle pâtés; cinnamon apple sponge cake, and strawberry-rhubarb pie. The Hofmann domestic staff, headed by Marie's personal servant, Hickey, would serve the food, and we would act as barmen, serving the liquors, champagne, and Bordeaux. As with so many society events, the party would begin following Mr. Hofmann's performance, around ten-thirty, and probably end sometime in the early morning hours.

There was another reason for Mrs. Hofmann's soiree. The year 1924 marked the fifth anniversary of the Fermata School for Girls,[30] which she founded in 1919, and many of the school's founding board members would be present.

In 1919, Mrs. Hofmann's daughter Josefa was thirteen years old. The Aiken Preparatory School had already been established by her cousin, Louise Hitchcock, three years prior, but it was primarily intended to educate boys. Believing that there was an equal need for budding debutantes, Marie began the Fermata School for Girls on the third floor of her Laurens Street home, Fermata. She enlisted the help of her best friend, Mary Curtis Bok, well known for her philanthropic generosity, who invested $5,000; Mr. Porter, a New York banker, invested $10,000; and husband Josef gave $3,000. Thus began the Fermata School with an opening enrollment of five students and four

---

30   The Fermata Tennis & Swim Club on Whiskey Road now occupies the gymnasium portion of the school. Its main building was razed following a fire during the WWII years.

instructors. In 1921, Marie's friend Mrs. C. Oliver Iselin joined her group of founders, and with a need for greater space due to a growing enrollment, the home and nine-acre estate of Col. Anthony R. Kuser of New Jersey, located on Whiskey Road, was bought and became the school's new location. By 1924, its fifth year of operation, Fermata had seventy boarders and twenty day students.

On the evening of the party, my Willcox staff and I were ready. We had set up three service bars, as well as a waitstaff that would meander throughout the home with sterling trays filled with bubbling flutes of Epernay's best champagne. Hickey and the Hofmanns' cook, Monroe, were directing the household staff in their preparations to serve the food.

The recital ended almost as planned except for the several encores with which Mr. Hofmann graced an enthusiastic and appreciative audience, who remained standing as they wildly applauded, following the sounding of the final note.

Guests began to arrive at eleven. Fermata's glittering, chandeliered hall had been decorated with floral arrangements of red roses and purple gladioli, interspersed with stands of forest fern and pink orchids. At thirty-four rooms Fermata easily qualified as a "cottage" with twelve rooms to spare. As guests streamed into the Louis XVI decorated parlor dominated by the black lacquered Steinway Concert Grand, in small intimate groups, the conversations glowed with admiration for Josef's virtuosic renditions of Beethoven's Moonlight Sonata and Debussy's Evening in Spain. Some couldn't decide if their favorite was Rachmaninoff's Prelude in C Sharp Major or Liszt's Venezia e Napoli. One thing was clear, Mrs. Hofmann's Pro Arte Society debut of 1924 began with one of the most memorable musical events to ever take place in Aiken. The opera house had been filled to capacity with local and finely dressed winter colony residents.

The staccato clink of metal on crystal was heard emanating from the drawing room entrance, which was immediately adjacent to the confluence of the hall and parlor, calling everyone to attention for an important announcement from Mrs. Hofmann.

"To all our guests, my sincerest thanks for joining us this evening for the debut of our Pro Arte Society, and special thanks to our dear friend Leopold Stokowski of the Philadelphia Orchestra for his kind introduction of my loving husband, Josef, and our Society."

The moment was then given to Mr. Stokowski, who proposed a toast "to my dear friend Josef, who has given Aiken, and indeed the world, a musical interpretation of the masters, equal to none since the time of Mozart."

Glasses were raised to a chorus of "Hear, hear!" He finished with the announcement that Mr. Pablo Casals had agreed to open next year's Pro Arte Society season, once again to be held at the Aiken Opera House.

THE REST OF THE STORY

Who could foretell from this elegant gathering of society's most genteel—where ostensibly, their hedonistic world was filled with the sunshine of spring, and storm clouds were forbidden—that unpleasant life changes for some who were gathered there would in the future come.

Within three years of the 1924 soiree, the marriage between Marie and Josef Hofmann would come to an end. Marie had long ago stopped accompanying Josef on his musical tours in order to spend time at home with Josefa. The stress and loneliness of touring Europe alone and the temptations that play on such situations became irresistible. Marie had been suspicious of Josef's wandering eye and his appreciation for the female form for some time, but she discounted much of what she'd heard to rumor and suppressed her persistent suspicions. Upon returning to Aiken from his musical tour, Christmas of 1926, Josef, in a heartbreaking meeting with his wife, discussed their deteriorating relationship and dour marital outlook.

In September 1927, he obtained a Swiss divorce and married a music student thirty years his junior.

Marie's life at Fermata could not continue, as it served as a reminder of happy memories there that were difficult to face. For a number of years she began spending summers in Bar Harbor, and the rest of the time in Europe. Her children were now grown and on their own, and Fermata's thirty-four rooms remained closed most of the time. The gaiety Marie had once shared with her winter colony friends was now a thing of the past. She was alone in her lackluster world, quietly contending with the continuing sorrow stemming from her broken marriage. At her sister Celestine's urging, she entered a sanatorium in Baltimore, which became her home for about ten years. Upon returning to Aiken, she found things had changed such that she could not resume the lifestyle she had previously known.

The 1927 demise of the Hofmann/Eustis marriage marked the end of Aiken performances by the renowned masters of the classical music world.

In 1927, Marie's best friend, Mary Curtis Bok's Curtis Institute of Music in Philadelphia had been operating for three years. It was in that year that Josef Hofmann[31] was made its third director and would remain in that position for twelve years. Leopold Stokowski was already a close friend of Mrs. Bok's at the time of the school's founding in 1924, and having "Stoki," as she called him, associated with the school served to mutually benefit the prestige of both the school and the Philadelphia Orchestra. With Hofmann now added to the faculty's administration, the Curtis Institute began to cultivate a reputation for attracting the

---

31   In November 1926, Hofmann became a U.S. citizen under the sponsorship of Mary Louise Curtis Bok.

most gifted students in the country and, indeed, the world. Over the years many of these graduates, like Leonard Bernstein, would go on to become icons in the music world, and a number of them would make a career with the Philadelphia Orchestra. Its faculty continued to attract some of the foremost names in music, such as Rudolph Serkin, Fritz Reiner, and Efrem Zimbalist, who would marry the school's founder, Mary Louise Curtis Bok, in 1943.

By the early 1930s, Hofmann had become an alcoholic, and in 1938, he left the Curtis Institute, a result of his drinking, marital problems, and a loss of interest in performing that caused his technical, artistic, and keyboard abilities to deteriorate. As a functioning alcoholic, and a debilitated image of his former genius, he lost the dependability of his virtuosic playing technique.

Although estranged from his daughter Josefa, Hofmann would write to her, and one would sense that his letters, while cordial, revealed an underlying soul that despite achieving the pinnacle of world-class musical career success was troubled, personally unfulfilled, and unhappy.

It has been reported that Sergei Rachmaninoff, a giant among Russian composers, in commenting on Hofmann in his later career said, "Hofmann is still sky high, the greatest pianist alive IF he is sober and in form. Otherwise, it is impossible to recognize the Hofmann of old."

Oscar Levant, screen composer and protégé of George Gershwin, wrote, "One of the terrible tragedies of music was the disintegration of Josef Hofmann as an artist. In his latter days, he became an alcoholic; his last public concert was an ordeal for all of us." His last public concert took place in 1946. Josef Hofmann died of pneumonia in Los Angeles on February 16, 1957.

EVALYN WALSH MCLEAN'S
REDEMPTION

The Lindbergh baby must be saved, I thought to myself as I sat in the darkness of my Hayne Avenue[32] Aiken home just as I did night after night at Fairview, my deceased mother's home outside of Washington. I was committed to my mission of saving the Lindbergh baby.

I was born in modest, some would even say poor, living circumstances, and, after acquiring great wealth and living an extravagant life, I now drew upon an innate sense of altruism long buried under the diamonds, homes, and excesses that had heretofore taken up my every living moment. I continued to wait in the darkness, as instructed, for the next stage of the plan.

It was on March 4, 1932 when I made contact with investigator and ex-FBI agent Gaston Means to intercede in the recovery of Colonel Lindbergh's kidnapped baby. Although I knew of Means' sleazy past, his reputation as a miscreant, and that he had spent time in federal prison, I thought that a man with his experience was needed to deal with these dreadful kidnappers. Moreover, he claimed to have connections to the kidnappers and knowledge of the baby's whereabouts.

Three days had passed since the baby was taken from his upstairs bedroom in the Lindberghs' home near Hopewell, New Jersey. Kidnappers demanded a $50,000 ransom, and by March 6th our national hero had received a second ransom note demanding $100,000. I mortgaged our Oxford property to raise the cash and advanced $100,000 plus expenses to Means, and by March 21st he had already

---

32   Each year Mrs. McLean leased an Aiken home on Hayne Avenue across from Mr. Pitkin's "Idylwood" at 918 Hayne Avenue, and next door to Dr. Harry Wilds' cottage at 739 Hayne. A brick wall now marks the area where Mrs. McLean's perennial rental once stood.

given the money over to his contact, known as the "Fox," a member of the kidnap gang.

Now I awaited the next set of instructions to meet and receive the child. I vigilantly sat, waited, and mused about my life.

As the nine-year-old[33] daughter of Thomas Walsh, a transplanted Irish immigrant turned miner, who had lived in many Colorado hotel rooms and rented shanties, I would never forget the day our lives changed in June 1896 when Father came home and exclaimed, "Daughter, I've struck it rich!" His perseverance in reexamining abandoned gold mines that had been given up as nonproductive paid off. One such mine, Camp Bird Gold Mine in Ouray, Colorado, began producing $5,000 per day in gold ore, making our family rich beyond our wildest dreams, or according to Father, "beyond the dreams of avarice." Mother, the former Carrie Bell Reed, a beautiful schoolteacher Father met in Leadville, was accustomed to a frugal lifestyle as we all were, but now we all, including my younger brother, Vinson, who I adored, were about to experience a dramatic change in lifestyle.

In 1897, we left Ouray for our new life in Washington, DC,[34] a city Father always admired. For six years we anxiously awaited the construction of our new abode, and in 1903, we moved into our new, sixty-room home at 2020 Massachusetts Avenue—the largest and most expensive[35] home in Washington. Father engaged the services of a New York architect, Mr. Henry Anderson, and asked that his design include a large staircase, similar to that of an ocean liner, and so he did design a grand, carved, Y-shaped mahogany staircase that ascended three floors, surrounded by an open deck promenade. The fourth floor included a ballroom and theater. The outside façade was of the Beaux-Arts style, and fit for royalty so much that in later years Father's friend King Leopold of Belgium and later King Albert became regular guests who

---

33   Evalyn Walsh was born in Leadville, Colorado, August 1, 1886.
34   Sources differ on the year the family moved to Washington. 1897 is used here as taken from *Queen of Diamonds*, Evalyn Walsh McLean's account of her life.
35   The home cost $835,000 to build in 1903.

both commented that our home compared with some of the castles of Europe.

My adolescent years at "twenty-twenty," as we called our new home, were a continuation of the mischievous, tomboy lifestyle that had early on become a personal characteristic of mine while growing up in Colorado. My brother Vinson was my frequent co-conspirator in many childhood escapades and pranks that we perpetrated on everyone who we thought would be fair game, especially our French governess. Now that we were in Washington and Father was becoming politically connected, it was felt that I should attend boarding school in New York to become "cultured." Why my parents thought that an expensive boarding school would work some magical formula and transform me I don't know, but I went. My time there was as harrowing for me as it was for the school, as I could not acclimate to them, nor they to me. I remember Father showing up one weekend at the school following a series of pining letters I had written. He took me out on the town to cheer me up. He asked me what I wanted, and I replied "Jewels," whereupon he took me to a jewelry store where I picked out a turquoise-and-seed-pearl dog collar, which I wore back to school and which was, like so many other things, against the rules. Little did I know that this introduction to jewelry would only whet my future appetite for some of the most luxurious jewels in the world. The following week, and after another caustic encounter with the Head Mistress, I called my brother Vinson to enlist his aid in breaking out of the place, and within a week I was back in Washington, never again to return to an American school. The remainder of my education took place at finishing school in Paris.

The rain had been falling off and on in Aiken for a week, something not unusual in early spring. Through the splattered raindrops on my front bay window I could see the blurred, streaky, twinkling headlights coming down Hayne Avenue. It was now 9:30 p.m. and I was thinking of Edward Jr., my fourteen-year-old and youngest son, who would be safely asleep by now at Aiken Preparatory School. He would normally be here with me, but during the school year he always boarded at the school. I didn't want him witness to the danger this night could bring.

Means said that he would arrive by 9:45 with the gang's leader to work out the exchange. I maintained my vigil.

I began to think about my life with Edward Beale (Ned) McLean, which could be summed up as an exhilarating, thrilling, heart-rending adventure through life, with a disastrous end. I first met Ned when we were both eleven years old. Our relationship was casual in those years as Ned grew into a gangly Washington teenager, where his father, John Roll McLean, was owner and publisher of two newspapers, *The Washington Post* and *The Cincinnati Enquirer*. Ned had been friends with my brother Vinson, who shared his love of fast driving and other thrill-seeking activities. Our relationship became closer following one of the most tragic events of my life.

It occurred on August 19, 1905 in Newport, Rhode Island, where Father had leased the Vanderbilt cottage for the summer. On that day Vinson and I had been to a luncheon at the Clambake Club, given by Mrs. Clement Moore. Our chauffeur, Emile Devoust, had driven us there in my new Mercedes. Following the luncheon, Vinson insisted on driving the car home. We left at about four in the afternoon, and true to form, Vin sped that Mercedes as if he were in a motor race, reaching speeds I would never dare to reach, and as we were recklessly flying down Honeyman's Hill we heard a pop, like a pistol shot, come from the rear tire as we approached the bridge. The car lurched and shook just before we struck the base and railing of the bridge. The last sounds I heard were cracking wood and scraping metal—then blackness, as I lay under the car, which was partially suspended by broken railing. I didn't know what happened to Vinson. At the hospital I learned that I had sustained a broken leg, and not until sometime later did I learn that Vinson had died at the scene, for the truth was kept from me. Everyone knew how close we were.

Following the accident, our family immediately returned to Washington, where we became recluse, and I lay in agony for weeks. It was during that time that Ned McLean came to visit, and each time he did, he brought new records for the Graphaphone[36] that played almost constantly in my room; a distraction from the pain. My leg refused to heal properly, and my parents' late night conversations about operations and surviving them that I overheard filled me with dread. It was Ned who told us about Dr. Finney, a great surgeon his father knew of who practiced at Johns Hopkins University. My father immediately called him, and that is how Ned McLean and I became close friends, which ultimately led to our marriage.

It was 10:00 p.m. and there was no sign of Means or the kidnappers. The rain continued to pour over Aiken in buckets, with brilliant, jagged lightning bolts lighting up Hayne Avenue, followed by sharp, ear-piercing thunder seemingly coming from just above our roof.

I'd just remembered the pen! In my anxiety I forgot to arm myself with the pen—the special pen loaded with poison. *Damn, where did I leave it? In the dresser drawer, the same drawer where I sometimes stash the cursed diamond—must get it now! Need to keep it with me—just in case!* My Aiken doctor friend[37] had loaded the pen with a special poison just as I had requested. If needed, it would be my first line of defense in a violent confrontation with the kidnappers. I'd never felt so insecure. With my marriage to Ned on the rocks, and *The Washington Post* heading into bankruptcy, I was alone in this as never before!

Our engagement was announced on July 4, 1908, and Ned's parents, of course, wanted a grand affair in Bar Harbor. But during a drive through Denver in July on a visit to our Colorado home, "Wolhurst," Ned just blurted, "Let's get married." I've always loved adventure and thought it was a good idea, and with a little help from our friend

---

36 Graphaphone was the name and trademark of an improved version of the phonograph invented at the Volta Laboratory established by Alexander Graham Bell in Washington, DC.

37 Mrs. McLean's memoir does not reveal who her Aiken doctor friend was, but her reference as to having been given a lethal pen at her request is very clear.

Crawford Hill, publisher of the *Denver Republican*, we carried it off with no fanfare.

Following our secret wedding ceremony on July 22nd at St. Mark's Episcopal Church in Denver, we left for a brief stay at the Antlers Inn in Colorado Springs.

Impromptu as our wedding was, that style was to become a repeating characteristic for a number of other events in our life together. No one was pleased of course with our "secret" elopement because it precluded an excuse for a society wedding, replete with luncheons, musicales, receptions, dinners, and dances. Despite our family being cheated out of a grand society wedding, Father gave me one hundred thousand dollars for honeymoon expenses. Mr. McLean matched the hundred thousand, so off we went touring Europe and the near Middle East, which proved to be a rollicking time. Our trip included a visit with the Sultan of Turkey, and an exception was made whereby I was allowed to visit his harem, which is where I first saw a most magnificent stone, what the world called the "Hope Diamond," being sported around the neck of one of the Sultan's favorites. While I was always interested in fine jewelry, an encounter at our last stop on the trip—Paris—began my love affair with world-class jewelry.

As it happened, on December 15th, I visited Cartier's at 13 rue de la Paix, owned by Pierre Cartier, a world-prominent jeweler who knew Father and got to know me during my Paris school days. Up to this point I had not bought my wedding gift, and, of course, Monsieur Cartier had just the thing for me. What he showed us was the most magnificent pendant dominated by a beautifully cut diamond he called "The Star of the East." I had never seen anything as beautiful, and I immediately realized how unique it must be. It consisted of a fine 94.80-carat pear-shaped diamond, mounted on a chain below a hexagonal emerald of thirty-four carats and a pearl of thirty-two grains, which, according to Cartier, might have belonged to the Sultan Abd al-Hamid

Cartier's price was 620,000 francs, or 120,000 dollars. Most of our honeymoon money was spent at this point, but because Mr. Cartier knew my father, we signed a document accepting the piece, and took home the Star of India. Our cash being low, we knew we didn't have enough to pay the duty on the diamond, so Ned smuggled the necklace into the country! Father later took care of the customs duty, pleading ignorance on our behalf, an excuse the customs officers accepted, or at least, Ned and I never heard anything further of it.

Pierre Cartier was a most interesting fellow, a great storyteller, and an astute businessman with a keen sense for recognizing a nascent sales opportunity. At the time of my purchase he had already, since 1906, opened a branch of his jewelry store in New York, and he also had one in London. I didn't see or hear from Monsieur Cartier again until Ned and I vacationed in Paris a few years later, where we stayed at the Hotel Bristol. Monsieur Cartier knew we were in town and asked if he could visit; he had a very special gem that he had recently acquired and wanted to show. When he arrived he opened a curious package revealing none other than the large blue diamond I had seen nearly three years earlier at the Sultan's harem. Cartier knew I had a love for excitement and risky adventures, and he had piqued my interest with his history of the stone—its past of misfortune and death for all who had possessed it (we later learned that the Sultan's woman who wore it was stabbed to death during the Turkish rebellion). Cartier's stories notwithstanding, while the stone was beautiful, I just didn't like the setting in which it was mounted.

It was in January 1911 that Monsieur Cartier showed up in Washington with the Hope, but now it had been re-set and attached to a necklace of smaller diamonds—simple but quite elegant. It was the most perfect blue diamond in existence, and I had to own it. So, in the executive offices of the *Washington Post*, where Ned had now assumed management from his father, a deal was made to purchase the Hope for $180,000. And while I didn't believe any of the tragedy and death stories resulting from a curse on those who possess the Hope, a clause was inserted into the purchase agreement that said, "Should any fatality occur to the family of Edward B. McLean within six months, the said Hope diamond is agreed to be exchanged for jewelry of equal value."

In 1920, Warren Harding, one of Ned's best friends, had been elected President, and Ned was made head of his inaugural committee. Oh, the many dinners, soirees, and musicales we hosted for hundreds of the top people in government and the military, where every extravagance was indulged and no expense spared. Ned and I sat atop the Washington social ladder, something Ned relished and of which he took full advantage, particularly when President Harding, his close friend and confidant, made him a member of the FBI, an official G-man, at the salary of $1 per year.

Life could not have been better from a material standpoint. We had built a new home that we called "Friendship," and we now owned Father's mansion at 2020 Massachusetts Avenue, another mansion in Georgetown, a 2,600-acre Belmont Farm in Virginia, an estate in Newport, and Briarcliffe in Bar Harbor, Maine. And as a consequence of Ned's passion for fine horses, we began spending winters here in Aiken, where the mild climate and the company of many of our equine-owning society friends made for a pleasant way to pass the winters. We even enrolled our sons Jock and Ned Jr. in the Aiken Preparatory School, where many of our friends also enrolled their children. However, our good fortune did not extend to the personal side.

Starting in 1916, my marriage to Ned had frayed to a large degree, and our public arguments were beginning to be noticed by friends and acquaintances. Our relationship was deteriorating. In May 1919, our nine-year-old son Vinson was struck and killed by a car as he played near the street in front of our home. We were away at the time, attending the races at Churchill Downs. Upon being notified, we rushed home, but Vinson died of a cerebral hemorrhage before we could arrive.

In 1920, Florence Harding, our new First Lady, became my close friend and confidant. Ned and Warren were frequently together, and absent from home much of the time. Florence and I shared our suspicions about our husbands' drinking, card playing, and philandering activities, and I even hired Gaston Means, a new acquaintance, to follow Ned in his daily wanderings. Means confirmed the worst. I didn't want to believe that the cursed Hope Diamond had anything to do with our misfortunes, but I couldn't deny that we had had more than our share of bad luck. By 1928, Ned and I were permanently living apart. I felt Ned's uncontrolled spending, chronic drunkenness, womanizing, and erratic behavior were driving him in the direction of madness, and I could only see a bad ending for him. Additionally, his outrageous spending was threatening to drive both the *Post* and the *Enquirer* over the financial edge.

I believe that tragedies in my family, from the death of my son Vinson to our impending financial ruin, would have happened whether I had owned the Hope Diamond or not. Perhaps a feeling of satisfaction and good in my mind and soul, in exchange for the self-centered and worthless feelings stemming from a profligate lifestyle for so many years, was the engine motivating me to not only help the Lindberghs now, but also guided my past efforts with Red Cross, and volunteer work during the Great War.

I was returned to reality by a sharp knock on the door. It was dark and the torrential rain continued to pour down on Aiken's streets, so much so that I could only see a faint outline of the Hahns' home across the street. There was a corpulent, bow-tied man on my doorstep wearing a dark fedora with water running off its brim as it would a spout on a measuring cup. I saw him through the spy hole, impatiently mashing a soggy cigarette underfoot. It was Gaston Means and he was not alone. A second man with him—thin, mustachioed, with an olive complexion as you would see in someone of Spanish descent—stood nervously at his side. He impatiently shook the rain to no relief from the collar of his dark, long London Fog, anxious for the door to open. He was a stranger. As I opened the door I was at once relieved that we might now have an outcome, and anxious, as I sensed something had gone wrong. The dour facial expressions coming through my doorway I was sure held a portent of bad news. The men smelled of tobacco and stunk of whiskey. They were breathing heavily as they recovered from the effects of walking the front steps in the cool downpour. I placed my hand in my pocket and cradled the poison pen, such small reassurance now, I felt, should something go wrong.

Without introducing his partner, Means began to speak as the Spanish-looking man, who said nothing, drilled me with a piercing, dark stare through his coal-black eyes. I unsuccessfully tried to avoid looking at his face, but my eyes were continually drawn to the ugly scar, looking almost like the side of a knife blade, which ran from the corner of his right eye almost to the bottom of his chin. One could only speculate, but it would seem that his was a terrible occu-pation. "I have bad news," began Means. "The child isn't here. He's been moved to Atlanta for safekeeping. It's the FBI; they're making our friends uncomfortable, so they were forced to quickly move him. We'll have to go there to make the exchange—and I will need more expense money."

With that statement the loudest thunder crack exploded above my home, and a jagged bolt of lightning flashed through the downpour, lighting up my living room and striking the large oak tree in the front yard, cleaving a limb the size of a phone pole and leaving a steaming black stump in its place. It was as if nature were sending its severest warning, or a portent of things to come. The Spanish-looking man be-gan to fidget while staring at me with a menacing eye. I thought of the Hope, wrapped in a stocking and hidden in the nearby gramophone speaker, and wondered whether his presence here was for more mali-cious purposes. As I stood there I began to doubt my ability to con-tinue my role in this situation. My mouth was dry—I had no spit. The moisture on Means' brow was now sweat, not raindrops, and he wore a dour expression while trying to be credible—I had my doubts even then, but of the pair he seemed the lesser of villains and was supposed to be working for me! My sweating hand closed hard on the secret poison pen in my pocket as my nerves ran amok.

With as firm a voice as I could muster I asked, "What about the money? I've given you over one hundred thousand dollars. How do I know we will ever receive the child?" As I spoke the words, my anger showed through, partly from nerves, partly from fear. I wasn't sure this night would end without harm to me or my property. I wondered if this was all a ruse. But I had to play along or risk everything! "All right, when and where should I be in Atlanta? I'll bring the expense money then—I don't have it here."

I gave my best stone-faced stare as I watched Means' eyes narrow and his lips purse. Clearly, he was upset about not receiving more expense money here and now. The Spanish-looking man's facial expression, like an eyelid-less snake, never changed. It was as if he was either deaf or didn't understand a word of English. I froze as he shoved his hand into his jacket pocket. I wasn't sure if I was about to be robbed or otherwise harmed. His wrist began to slowly emerge from the pocket, and much to my relief his hand held a pack of cigarettes, whereupon he quickly tapped one out.

"I will call you with the Atlanta details tomorrow. Be sure to have four thousand more with you," said Means. Not another word was uttered as they pivoted, opened the door, and walked out into the nighttime torrent. I watched them turn and drive away toward town as the windblown rain in streaked waves washed across Hayne Avenue in their vehicle's wake.

With a shaking hand I filled a glass with bourbon, relieved to conclude this stage of my bizarre transaction, but reliving the words and expressions of dangerous men.

The man accompanying Gaston Means that night in Aiken was later identified only as the "King of the Kidnappers." He was never seen again, and his real identity never became known. Evalyn Walsh McLean was lured to Atlanta by Gaston Means in her mission to obtain the kidnapped child, only to be asked for an additional thirty-five thousand dollars, and to go to still another location in Mexico to receive the child. Failing to raise the money, and suspecting a scam, she asked for all her money back, whereupon Means, ever the con man, attempted to play her along. She contacted the police and Gaston Means was eventually captured by the FBI. He was ultimately found guilty of grand larceny and sentenced to serve fifteen years in a federal penitentiary. Mrs. McLean never received a dollar of her money. Means died in Leavenworth Prison in 1938.

The search for the Lindbergh infant ended on May 12, 1932, when the remains of an infant were discovered about two miles from the Lindberghs' home in the woods near a road just north of the small village of Mount Rose, New Jersey. Lindbergh identified the child's body as that of his kidnapped son.

On October 31, 1933, Ned McLean was declared insane by a jury in Maryland, following which he was committed indefinitely to a psychiatric hospital in Towson, Maryland. He died of a heart attack on July 28, 1941 at Shepard-Pratt Sanitarium, where he had been confined.

Evalyn Walsh McLean died on April 26, 1947 at the age of sixty of pneumonia, and was buried in Rock Creek Cemetery, Washington, DC, in the Walsh family tomb.

Following Mrs. McLean's death, the Hope Diamond was sold to pay the debts of her estate. Her newspapers, *The Washington Post* and *The*

Cincinnati Enquirer, had already been sold at bankruptcy auction prior to her death.

In 1949, New York jeweler Harry Winston purchased Evalyn's collection and sent the Hope Diamond on a nine-year goodwill tour around the United States to raise money for charity. Wherever it went, news reports with stories of its notorious past aroused curiosity and magnified its legend. In 1958, in an effort to help develop a major national gem collection for the American people, Winston donated the gem to the Smithsonian Institution. Today the diamond resides in the museum's Hall of Geology, Gems and Minerals, stately revolving behind three inches of bulletproof glass in the Harry Winston Room.

Aiken Map

1. **Hitchcock Home**
   (not extant)
2. **Hofmann Home**
   (not extant)
3. **McLean Home**
   (not extant)
4. **Whitney Home**
   (extant)
5. **Kuser Home**
   (not extant/modified)
6. **Vanderbilt Home**
   (not extant)

(author's map)

Louise & Thomas Hitchcock with hounds. Drag hunts through the preserve were generally held on Thursdays and Saturdays.
(Courtesy of Aiken County Historical Museum)

Louise Hitchcock astride her favorite mount, Cavalier, clearing a jump at one of the many equine events held during the season.
(Courtesy of Aiken County Historical Museum)

Mon Repos, the Hitchcock's Laurens Street home where
Louise spent her last three months in a second floor bedroom.
(Courtesy of Aiken County Historical Museum)

George A. Durban, Jr., took his place in his
father's bond, insurance, and real estate
business following graduation from Clemson
College in 1937. Since his school days he was
involved in the management of a number
of wealthy winter colonists' estates, such as
the W.R. Grace estate, overseeing them during
the off season. *(Photo Courtesy of the Durban family)*

"Fermata," the Hofmann's thirty-four room home on Laurens Street served as the Fermata School for Girls when opened with five students in 1919. (Public Domain)

Originally opened in 1898 by Frederick Willcox at the urging of Louise Hitchcock, the Willcox Inn played host to many of the Rich and Famous visitors to Aiken such as the Lorillards, Winston Churchill, FDR, John Jacob Astor, William Vanderbilt, Elizabeth Arden, Horace Dodge, Fred Astair to name a few. The Willcox continues to operate as the luxury hotel of Aiken to this day. (Public Domain)

Josef Hofmann child prodigy
circa 1890 (*George Grantham Bain
Collection, Library of Congress*)

Josef Hofmann reached the
international pinnacle of
musical success when he
married Marie Eustis in 1905.
In 1927 they divorced, and
his career began a slow
decline. (*Public Domain*)

Leopold Stokowski of the Philadelphia Orchestra, and Curtis Institute fame, was a friend of the Hofmanns, and a winter visitor to Aiken. *(Wikimedia Commons/Public Domain)*

In 1921The Fermata School for Girls moved to its new location on Whiskey Road (hwy. 19), in the former home of Colonel Anthony R. Kuser. By 1924 it had 90 students. *(Courtesy of Aiken County Historical Museum)*

Walsh family early photo. (L to R) Vinson Walsh, who died in the prime of his youth;Thomas Walsh, Irish immigrant carpenter turned gold mine millionaire; Carrie Bell Reed Walsh, family matriarch; Evalyn Walsh, who would marry into the McLean newspaper dynasty.
(Public Domain)

Mr. & Mrs. Edward "Ned" Beale McLean. Ned was always better at spending money rather than making it. Evalyn enjoyed jewelry and entertaining society and political figures at her Washington home. Pictured here with her dogs, she was an animal lover, and had many pets throughout her life.
(Library of Congress/unrestricted use)

Evalyn Walsh McLean wearing the Hope Diamond. When not wearing it she would wrap the gem in a stocking and store it in the speaker of her gramaphone at her Aiken home.
In Washington she had the diamond fitted into a dog collar for her Great Dane, Mike, who would trot out and display it for certain guests.
(Harris & Ewing Collection/Library of Congress)

Dinsmore Cottage on Hayne Avenue was Mrs. McLean's perennial Aiken rental. *(Public Domain)*

Gaston Means, ex-FBI agent turned con man, swindled $100,000 from Mrs. McLean while posing as a confidant of the Lindbergh baby kidnappers. His ruse, designed to extract more cash from her, took the form of delays and meetings in Washington, Aiken, Atlanta, with a final change of venue to Mexico when she reported him to federal authorities.

Means was convicted and died in Leavenworth Prison in 1938.
(National Photo Collection, Library of Congress)

William C. Whitney circa 1885 when he
served as Secretary of the Navy.
His love for race horses grew alongside his
rise in the world of politics and business. In
1892 he bought Aiken's first polo field and
encircled it with a race track to run his
thoroughbreds. He was a very well known
figure at Saratoga Springs, New York, and
Argenteuil, France where he regularly
attended races.

Along with his friend, Thomas Hitchcock, he
introduced golf to the southeast with the
building of Aiken's famed Palmetto Golf Club,
one of the oldest golf clubs in the U.S.
(photo Public Domain)

Flora Payne married William C. Whitney in 1869.
Her father was a politician, lawyer and involved
in railroad development. Her brother became
very wealthy as a partner in John D. Rockefeller's
Standard Oil Company.
For a number of years Whitney labored under
the nagging insecurity that all he had was bought
with his brother-in-law and father-in-law's money,
a public perception that he was dedicated to
changing. *(Public Domain)*

Edith Randolph Whitney was the widow of a Brtitish military man, Captain Arthur Randolph of the Queen's Own Hussars.

She met William Whitney during summers at Bar Harbor, Maine, and they were married in a quiet ceremony in September 1896. Their marriage was to draw the ire of Whitney's former brother-in-law, Oliver Payne, who considered the marriage an insult to the memory of his sister, Flora. The schism he created within the family turned two of Whitney's children against him, and lasted until his death in 1904.

In 1898 Edith was to suffer a serious riding accident in Aiken which would ultimately claim her life *(Photo Public Domain)*

Joye Cottage at sixty rooms was one of Whitney's more modest homes. There were twenty-four rooms for guests in addition to the servants' quarters, billiard room, and reception hall which measured thirty-six by forty feet. Whitney's additions to the property were a two-tiered squash court and racing stables containing thirty-two stalls, eight standing stalls, with additional room for twenty-two vehicles.
(Courtesy of Aiken County Historical Museum)

Colonel Oliver Hazard Payne served in the Union army and later became very wealthy from his involvement in the formation of American Tobacco Trust, U.S. Steel, and treasurer of John D. Rockefeller's Standard Oil Company.

He was extremely protective of his sister, Flora, and developed an intense hatred for Whitney following his sister's death and Whitney's subsequent marriage. *(Public Domain)*

Dorothy Payne Whitney Straight remained loyal to her father following the family schism initiated by her uncle, Oliver Hazard Payne.

She was to marry Willard Straight, a U.S. diplomat based in the far east.
(Assoc. of Junior Leagues Intl./ unrestricted)

John Fairfield Dryden, Founder of Prudential Financial and Anthony Kuser's father-in-law.

Upon his death in 1911 his daughter, Susan Fairfield Dryden Kuser inherited $50 million. *(Public Domain)*

"Tall Pines" was the Kuser home on Whiskey Road (hwy. 19) in Aiken.
Colonel Kuser was a naturalist and a dog lover. He was an early member of Aiken's famed Palmetto Golf Club, and made a portion of his property available for the building of the Palmetto's second clubhouse.

His son John and wife Brooke were also winter guests. Brooke would eventually marry Vincent Astor and become famed socialite, Brooke Astor. (Public Domain)

Los Incas, the Kuser home in Palm Beach.
(Public Domain)

William Kissam Vanderbilt was the grandson of Commodore, Cornelius Vanderbilt, founder of the family dynasty.
His marriage to the socially ambitious Alva Smith Vanderbilt ended in 1895 amid accusations of infidelity.

In 1903 he married Anne Harriman Sands Rutherfurd Vanderbilt to whom he was devoted for the remaining seventeen years of his life.

He died following a heart attack which occurred while at the races at Auteuil, France in 1920. His body was returned to New York where he was buried at the family's mausoleum at New Dorp on Staten Island.
(Public Domain)

Willie K. Vanderbilt, Jr. was a race car enthusiast, a sport to which he was devoted until his second marriage. His first wife, Virginia Fair Vanderbilt ,was the heir to the famous "Comstock Lode" silver mine fortune established by her father. She bore Willie three children, and by 1908 she and Willie were estranged.

In 1927 he married Rosamund Lancaster Warburton. Abandoning auto racing, he and Rosamund spent much of their time cruising the world aboard his yacht.

Willie's son, Willie III, inherited his father's love for cars and racing. He was killed in an auto accident in South Carolina in 1933.
(Public Domain)

"Elm Court" the Vanderbilt home located on the corner of Colleton Avenue and Union Street in Aiken. William K. Vanderbilt bought the home from his second wife, Anne's family, the wealthy and prominent Harrimans of New York. Anne was an avid horsewoman, and William shared her love for horses and riding. They split their time between New York, Aiken, and Poissy, France, where William also maintained riding stables. *(Courtesy of Aiken County Historical Museum)*

Harold S. "Mike" Vanderbilt was the youngest of William's children. He was noted for his yachting and love of games, especially contract bridge, which he invented.
He served for many years on the board of Vanderbilt University.
(Public Domain)

WILLIAM C. WHITNEY'S
REUNION AT JOYE COTTAGE

As the cool morning breeze wafts through my bedroom window I awaken to the scent of pine and the sounds of spring. It is so good to be back in Aiken and at Joye Cottage. My dear friend William Whitney has once again included me in his travels. We have had so many good times together, particularly since poor Flora's[38] passing.

For some time and certainly toward the last years of their marriage, Will[39] and Flora had become distant, with each pursuing their own interests and diversions. Flora didn't give a whit for horse racing or running with the hounds, and I feel sure she would have found Aiken not to her liking, had she lived longer. Her milieu was the sumptuous gatherings of the 400 in New York's biggest and most beautiful mansions, including her own at the corner of Fifth Avenue and Fifty-Seventh Street, a wedding gift from her brother, Oliver.[40] For his part, Will constantly labored under the nagging insecurity that all he had was bought with his brother-in-law and father-in-law's money, a public perception that he was dedicated to changing.

Flora Payne was born in 1848 to Henry B. and Mary Perry Payne of Cleveland, Ohio. Henry Payne had been a lawyer with a thriving practice in Cleveland until health issues forced him to leave the legal profession and become a businessman and politician. While serving on Cleveland's city council, he became involved in railroad issues and acquired a great deal of knowledge about that industry. It was from

---

38   Flora Payne of Cleveland, Ohio, married William C. Whitney of New York in 1869. She died February 5, 1893.

39   He was also known as "W.C."

40   Col. Oliver Hazard Payne served in the Union Army and later became very wealthy from his involvement in the formation of American Tobacco Trust, U.S. Steel, and as treasurer of Rockefeller's Standard Oil Company.

this involvement that his later business interest was in railroad development. Additionally, he was a business partner with John D. Rockefeller in the Standard Oil Company and an Ohio State senator. This is the elite environment within which Flora was raised. However, unlike the typical, passive-submissive, marginally educated society debutante of the day, her energetic personality, powered by a Cambridge education that placed her on an equal, intellectually intimidating footing with her potential suitors, is possibly the reason why she was still uninvolved[41] as she approached her twentieth year. That perhaps provided the motivation for Oliver to visit his old Yale friend, William Whitney, who was then[42] practicing law on Wall Street with former classmate Henry Dimock.

Oliver had been two years ahead of Will at Yale. They weren't particularly close, but both were members of Yale's Skull and Bones. Following Yale, Oliver joined the Union Army, attained the rank of colonel, and distinguished himself at the battle of Chickamauga, where he was wounded, ending his military career. Conversely, following Yale, Will had gone on to Harvard Law School, where he spent two years before beginning his legal career. The two had not seen one another since the Yale college days, yet on a business trip to New York, Oliver paid a visit to renew the friendship, which I believe was motivated by his desire to see his sister become attached to the "right" man and avert what appeared to him to be the inevitable march to spinsterhood.

It was such a short time ago that I lay in one of Will's guestrooms in his New York mansion recovering from my heart ailment. Now I sense Will knows that my health falters, and this may be the last time I'm able to visit his beloved winter refuge. In this first year of the new century, everyone is filled with optimism, an optimism I cannot appreciate in my diminished state of health. I never shared Will's love for equestrian activities, but apart from that, my physician has cautioned

---

41   She did have one involvement with a young man who was deemed unsuitable by her parents, who sent her off on an extended European grand tour in order to derail this dangerous liaison.

42   1867

me to pass the time in rest and exercise consisting of measured walks in the company of a nurse; therefore, taxing equestrian activities would be out of the question, even if I did share that interest.

Equestrian sports aside, Will and I have been kindred spirits in all other things since I first met him, under the most somber conditions, while traveling with Oliver to Europe in the summer of 1883. That summer, Flora had left for Europe with the Whitney children, Harry, William, Pauline, and five-year-old Olive. Will remained in New York to attend to political and business commitments. It was in Paris on June 5th that little Olive, having contracted diphtheria, tragically died after a short illness. Flora had been accompanied there by a friend, Ellen Hopkins; otherwise, she was alone to deal with the situation until family could arrive.

Immediately upon being cabled, Will took the seven-day voyage to Paris, fearing that his other children, or Flora, would fall victim to the same disease. Oliver, who adored his sister, immediately joined her, and I, a longtime Payne family friend, accompanied Oliver. It was under this melancholic circumstance that I met[43] my greatest friend, William C. Whitney.

My father, Alexander Gunn, for whom I was named, was a highly successful merchant in Cleveland. After enjoying a privileged child-hood and benefitting from a classical education, I inherited what my father had built, and operated my hardware business before selling out and retiring in 1879. At that time I was seized by a desire to change my life in a most radical way. I turned to a simple and contempla-tive life by joining a group of breakaway German Lutheran separatists in Tuscarawas County, Ohio, in a communal village called Zoar. We were known as Zoarites, and not unlike the Amish of Pennsylvania, we were self-sustaining and simple in our lifestyle. Unlike my Zoar brethren, however, I still appreciated the finer things I had known in

---

43   Gunn had originally met Whitney in 1874 but had not seen him or engaged him as a friend until this event in 1883.

my previous lifestyle: world classics, travel, fine wines and champagne. While these things were still important to me, I simultaneously had an ongoing desire for intellectual and spiritual contentment, which I thought could be found and ideally nurtured in the Zoar environment. It had been my previous business connections that brought me into contact with Flora Payne's family, and particularly her brother, Oliver. I was a Zoarite when I became reacquainted with William C. Whitney.

My attention is drawn by a gentle knock at my chamber door, followed by the soft but firm, aristocratic, baritone voice of Will's head butler, Regan,[44] announcing that breakfast is being served in the main dining room. I dress hurriedly and head downstairs as I know Will, being an early riser, will soon be out meeting his fellow Aiken equestrians at his racetrack and polo field.[45] He recently paid $60,000 for "Hamburg,"[46] the second highest amount ever paid at auction for a thoroughbred, and he is anxious to get him out on the track. Of course, as the grandson of the famous "Hindoo,"[47] and son of "Hanover,"[48] Hamburg is far more valuable as a stud, siring potential winners, than racing around Will's Aiken track. Since I know it is his habit to play golf in the afternoon at the Palmetto Golf Club[49] following his time at the track, I don't want to miss him at breakfast. Otherwise, I won't see him until tonight's musicale in the Joye Cottage ballroom, where Will has engaged a young Catalan cellist by the name of Pablo Casals to play for his guests.

Will's love of racehorses grew alongside his rise in the world of

---

44   Thomas Regan was Whitney's loyal secretary for many years and, upon Whitney's death, continued to serve his son, Harry Payne Whitney.

45   Whitney Field, Aiken's first polo field built in 1882, was bought by William C. Whitney in 1892. Whitney added the racetrack encircling the field after he purchased it.

46   (1885-1915) With eleven major wins in 1897, he was the leading American colt of his generation and American Horse of the Year in 1898.

47   (1878-1901) He won thirty of his thirty-five starts, including the Kentucky Derby, the Travers Stakes, and the Clark Handicap.

48   (1884-1899) He won his first seventeen races and was leading American Stallion sire for four consecutive years.

49   Whitney and his friend Thomas Hitchcock initiated the construction of Aiken's Palmetto Golf Club when they built the first four holes in 1892.

politics and business. He was born in Conway, Massachusetts, in 1841. His father, General James S. Whitney, was a Democratic activist and a member of the Massachusetts House of Representatives. Will would eventually emulate his father's political activism, but unlike his father, Will would command a much larger political stage, and commensurately that involvement would bring him into contact with people who would further his rise in the business world and, consequently, the opportunity for great wealth in his own right.

It was his law practice in New York and two high-profile cases that he was successfully involved in that attracted attention and first gave rise to a reputation that would grow and place him in view of New York's most influential political players. Subsequently, in 1871, he and other prominent Democrats established the Young Men's Democratic Club of New York, a group dedicated to promoting honesty in government at a time when corrupt politics was the norm in New York City. In 1875, he was appointed city attorney, a job that paid $15,000 per year, and began to systematically defeat or settle the many suits brought through the corruption that had been prevalent in New York City politics. This was followed in 1876 by his being appointed delegate to the Democratic National Convention in St. Louis, where he stood shoulder to shoulder with the most influential (and wealthy) individuals in New York. Clearly, Will was "on his way."

As we are seated for breakfast, I see familiar faces but am somewhat startled. All present are equestrian acquaintances and family members who I've met here before. I say startled because the event that took place on our last meeting at Joye Cottage inflicted a lasting sorrow and sadness upon us all, but most of all upon Will. It has been two years, since 1898, that I've seen this particular group of Will's friends: Lady and Sir Edward Colebrooke, the British Liberal Party leader, and also from England, Sydney Paget, Will's son-in-law's brother; Adelaide Randolph, his stepdaughter; Dorothy Whitney, his daughter; and a New York physician friend, Dr. C. F. McGahan. It defies coincidence that this exact same guest configuration should be present here together, the same group who witnessed an equestrian tragedy slightly over two years ago.

Amidst the handshakes and cheek kisses, and as each guest makes their renewal of friendship, I notice that before each place is set a small envelope with each person's name written in a fine script. Like the others, I immediately open my envelope and remove the elegant card, which contains the following handwritten message:

> *I am sorry for not being able to join you for breakfast this morning, as each of you holds a special place in my heart. I have thought of all of you often over the past two years, and I would be grateful if you would join me in the Joye Cottage library at four o'clock this afternoon for refreshments. With warmest regards, Will*

As the guests read their cards, each looks to the other questioningly, but unspoken, about what purpose Will's meeting will hold. Without a word each knows the significance of the timing for being present now at Joye Cottage, and the special relationship they've shared since that fateful day in 1898. They also know that more than refreshments will be in store, as everyone knows that Will is a purposeful man.

The extended silence is broken by Baron Colebrooke. "I say, Gunn, how has the world treated you these past two years?" he asks, using his finest British military brogue acquired during his years as captain of the Honourable Corps of Gentlemen-at-Arms, and in the company of many royal Scotsmen.

I know his question is more rhetorical than sincere, but I decide to give a naïve, honest response. "I've had some health issues, which continue to plague me, but I was able to do a bit of traveling to Europe, and New York to visit Will," I respond candidly. "I'm under complete rest orders from my doctor, so I won't be very active during this visit,"

I add.

"Then I suppose you won't be up for some squash," Colebrooke sniffs as he sips his morning tea. "We were counting on you to join us for a few sets. We've been anxious to give Will's new squash court a try after breakfast. We'll miss you, old sport."

"May I join you for a morning walk, Mr. Gunn?" asks Dorothy. "The weather this morning is so beautiful, and I promise to be as helpful as the nurse who would usually accompany you."

"Thank you, Dorothy. That would be delightful. Let's meet on the piazza at ten sharp," I say as I rise to return to my room to finish morning ablutions.

As I sit awaiting Dorothy in one of the many pine green rockers that, like a row of soldiers, are perfectly aligned on the sweeping front piazza, I think about how my relationship with Dorothy strengthened with the advent of Will's marriage to Edith Randolph, his second wife.

Edith was the widow of a British military man, Captain Arthur Randolph of the Queen's Own Hussars. They had been married from 1878 until his death about seven years later. During the marriage she had spent some time living in Europe and later, following his death, in Bar Harbor, Maine and New York. That is when she met my friend Will. It was later, on a trip to London with his wife, Flora, his sister, and brother-in-law Charles Barney, that Will again encountered the widowed Edith Randolph. He was so bored with his Flora/Barney companions that he took to an escapade with Edith, which included a shopping and sightseeing spree, leaving his familial group for an impolite period of time. This incident would inflame the preexisting enmity between him and Flora and, like a canker, would fester with Flora for a time to come. Flora had always been suspicious of Will's affable manner around women, and often accused him of having other than honorable intentions with female acquaintances. Mrs. Randolph was at the top of her list.

There certainly was some ongoing attraction between Will and Mrs.

Randolph because in September 1896, three years after Flora's death, they were married in a quiet ceremony. Will would have had the opportunity to see Edith at Bar Harbor, where they both were perennial summertime visitors, the same place their engagement was announced, so today, Will's behavior with Edith Randolph is a moot question for some, but not for everyone.

When the marriage took place, I offered them my best wishes, as I loved them both dearly. This feeling was shared by Dorothy, who was a precocious nine years old at the time, and her brother Harry,[50] who had married Gertrude Vanderbilt[51] only one month prior. However, Will's marriage to Edith would bring about a great schism in the Payne/Whitney family, with Oliver Payne's condemnation of the union as an affront to his sister's memory. Oliver's vitriol was used to recruit Will's son Payne[52] and daughter Pauline[53] to his camp with a promise of a great Payne inheritance[54] in return for repudiating their father. I became a part of that schism as my warm and compassionate relationship with Will and Edith caused the dissolution of my longtime friendship with Oliver. I can no longer be in his presence lest I risk raising his most caustic ire.

I am returned from my musing by the sound of tension from the stretched spring of the screen door, followed by the sound of Dorothy's voice. "Well, Mr. Gunn, are you ready for our walk?" she asks with a youthful rhythm to her voice. "Shall we head in the direction of the Hitchcocks[55] and down the hill toward the preserve[56]?" she asks gingerly.

---

50 Harry Payne Whitney was W.C. Whitney's eldest son, born in 1872.

51 Gertrude Vanderbilt was the eldest surviving daughter of Cornelius Vanderbilt II, born in 1875.

52 Payne's first name was William after his father, but after the family schism he dropped the William and was known only as Payne Whitney.

53 Pauline was William Whitney's eldest daughter, born in March 1874.

54 Oliver Payne's wealth, primarily gained as a John D. Rockefeller partner, was immense, and considerably outweighed Whitney's very substantial wealth.

55 Thomas and Louise Hitchcock were close Whitney friends and were responsible for Whitney's discovery of Aiken as a winter equine playground.

56 The preserve was part of an 8,000-acre forest that the Hitchcocks and Whitneys jointly purchased for fox hunting and other equine activities. It would ultimately be called Hitchcock Woods.

"That's a great plan, let's visit the preserve," I respond as I admire her handsome features.

As we walk in silence from Easy Street toward Laurens, I can't help noticing how she has physically matured since the terrible accident in the preserve two years ago. She has grown up quickly. My thoughts go back to her christening at St. John's Church on Lafayette Square, in Washington, DC, April of 1887. At the time, Will was serving as Secretary of the Navy, having been appointed by President Cleveland in 1885. Will's Democratic political activities in New York had raised his visibility and importance within the party, so much so that he became a significant player in Grover Cleveland's election. In return, the new president appointed him Secretary of the Navy, a post in which he was to excel and receive recognition. Under his direction the U.S. Navy was modernized and raised to a readiness level it hadn't seen since the early days of our republic. His success at this point in his career notwithstanding, he was still dependent upon Payne largess, particularly from brother-in-law Oliver, whose love of and devotion to family made him more than willing to share the wealth. While Will's financial fortunes were on the rise, he had not yet arrived. However, Flora was unconcerned as she found Washington a fresh alternative to New York society, and a new and grand environment within which to entertain and be entertained by the rich and powerful.

"Halloo...halloo there, Alexander and Dorothy!" We hear someone calling from the direction of Mon Repos.[57] As we approach closer we can see Louise Hitchcock through the clusters of bloomed camellias, standing on the veranda of her home, calling as she waves to us.

"Why hello, Mrs. Hitchcock," says Dorothy. "It has been a long time since last seeing you. I hope you are well."

"We're all fine here," returns Louise. "How is your father? Tell him we look forward to joining him this evening for the musicale."

---

57   Mon Repos was the home of Louise and Thomas Hitchcock located at the top of the hill, at the end of Laurens St.

"I will be glad to do so," replies Dorothy.

"Oh, and please tell him that we are in full agreement with the proposal for handling the preserve, and that we would like to finalize the details soon," adds Louise.

"Yes, I'll be sure to pass it on to him. We look forward to seeing you this evening, Mrs. Hitchcock," says Dorothy.

We approach the Laurens Street entrance to the preserve, and begin down one of the familiar paths that Will and the others have ridden many times. As we walk we can hear the nearby rustling of underbrush created by animal inhabitants taking cover at our approach. It is particularly beautiful today, with new pin oak foliage glittering in the morning spring sunshine. We take a turn, continue on for another few minutes, and follow a path that leads past a small bridge spanning a ravine bordered by wild dogwoods; a white one blooming here, a pink there, randomly scattered, but scattered in an aesthetically delightful way. Autumn leaves still cover the ground, but their brown monotony is broken here and there by new, wild green sprigs and pine straw, long fallen from the many long leaf pines nearby. Climbing Yellow Carolina Jessamine encircles and decorates the rough lower timbers of the small bridge in their steady climb, which is already well underway. The faint glistening evidence of the morning's dew is almost gone as it outlines the ancient scars marking the lower timber supports of the bridge.

Such a scene of quiet, natural serenity, which could serve as a model of springtime beauty for the artist's canvas, disguises the scene of a horrific accident that took place here only two years earlier.

"It happened here," says Dorothy as she looks away from the bridge and turns to me with a grave look upon her face. "It was on February twenty-first, two years ago, and I remember it as if it had taken place yesterday. We had just left the Hitchcocks' cottage, and they were joining us for a ride through the preserve. The Colebrooks; my stepsister, Adelaide Randolph; Sidney Paget; Dr. McGahan; my stepmother, Edith; and Father were all in the group. The Hitchcocks' stable boy had captured a deer, and for sport, we were intent on pursuing it as it was being released into the wild. The chase came down this very path with the deer outpacing our mounts with its graceful leaps and bounds. It ran into this ravine and under the bridge with all of us in hot pursuit. As we approached the bridge, we spread out somewhat so those passing under could all remain within the confines of the bridge supports. We were all familiar with the space limitations under this bridge as we all had been through here many times before. We knew that in order to successfully make it through, the rider would need to bend his head to his horse's nape in order to avoid hitting the wooden bridge trusses."

"On this particular day we all rode our regular mounts except for Edith. Her mare was being shod that morning, so she rode a larger gelding that was at least two hands higher than her usual mount. She knew she had to bend to avoid the bridge support timbers, but did not account for the larger mount she was riding and failed to clear the wooden under-support of the bridge. She struck her head and was thrown to the ground. Adelaide, who was in the rear, began to shriek as she dismounted and ran to her mother's side. Father, who was ahead, wheeled his mount upon hearing Adelaide's cries, and raced back to the bridge. I could see his eyes wide and mouth agape as he yelled Edith's name upon seeing her prone figure under the bridge. I was riding almost astride Edith, and I will never forget the hollow, dull thud of the impact, her head jerking back, leading her body to the ground behind her still-running mount. Dr. McGahan, upon hearing the cries, was quick to leap from his mount and run to Edith as she lay under the bridge, unmoving, blood flowing from her nose, a slashed scalp, and a black bruise already beginning to form at the place of impact. She was unconscious and had a shallow breath as McGahan attended her. Adelaide was hysterical and was uncomforted by my embrace as we both sobbed heavily. Father knelt by her side and took her hand in his in a helpless effort to comfort. Sidney rode to the cottage to fetch the wagon to transport the comatose Edith home. Eighteen months she lingered, paralyzed, conscious, and at times unconscious, until she died."

I can see tears begin to well as Dorothy struggles with the memory of the accident and it saturates what is left of her emotional equilibrium. I place my arm around her shoulder to comfort and say, "Let's head back to the cottage, Dorothy. We've had enough exercise for one day."

We walk home in silence.

Upon arrival at the cottage, Dorothy goes straight to her room, I'm sure to regain some sense of composure. I decide to forego lunch and take a nap in my room before our four o'clock meeting in the library with Will.

I awaken at three o'clock, surprised at the length and depth of my sleep, no doubt brought on by my debilitated health. It takes little time for me to prepare for this evening's activities, and I think I will explore Will's cottage a bit.

Will's Aiken home consists of sixty rooms: twenty-four rooms for guests in addition to servants' quarters, billiard room, and reception hall. It is perhaps the most modest of his homes when compared to his palaces in New York City, Old Westbury, Bar Harbor, and Lenox, Massachusetts. It was following his marriage to Edith that he began spending large sums of money making her as comfortable as possible. At that time he completed his quarter mile of stable at the Westbury home, for she was an avid horsewoman. Here in Aiken, his billiard room is sumptuous, and his reception hall measures a voluminous thirty-six by forty feet. The entire home is outfitted with the most unique and valuable antiques that Will's agents have gathered from throughout the country and Europe. The home is of a Southern colonial design, with sweeping verandas that are only interrupted by columns set every four feet or so, extending up two stories. The stable, which contains thirty-two stalls, eight standing stalls, with still room left for twenty-two vehicles, is enormous at two stories in height. The stable architecturally matches the home. He recently added the squash court, which in itself is an impressive building.

Will's collection of homes and racehorses was made possible through his success in consolidating and controlling the street car business in New York City. Of course, inheriting his wife's money helped as well.

The street car lines in New York at the time of Will's rise within the city and state Democratic Party were fragmented and owned by a number of independent interests. Through business acumen, political connections, and recruiting the right men as business partners, he was able to buy and consolidate the various lines under one business umbrella controlled by him and his partners. At one point his business owned over six thousand horses, used to pull those cars through the streets of New York City. He sold stock in his "Traction" company, as it was called, and managed, on a number of occasions, to run up the price, sell out, and reap the gains. He did this a number of times and drew criticism for what some thought were unethical business practices. By 1895, he had become quite wealthy in his own right. But now, combined with the inherited Payne money, he is one of the wealthiest men in the country. That is, after his brother-in-law, Oliver, the Rockefellers, and a very few others.

I notice that it is nearing four o'clock, so I proceed to the library for the meeting with Will. On the way I am met by the Colebrooks and Dr. McGahan, who are also headed in the same direction. Regan meets everyone at the library entrance and directs us to our seats. The library is outfitted with antique furniture gathered from around the world. Persian rugs cover the floor, and the room is lit by electric lights, an innovation Will has recently installed. The massive fireplace, which dominates the room, is crowned by a large white marble mantel adorned with cherubs and scrolls beginning at its edges and traversing its entire length. Will obtained the fireplace and mantel from a chateau in the Loire valley and had it transported here and reassembled. The ceiling, some thirty feet above, is decorated with images of mythic beings, more cherubs, and bordered in gold gilt. We can smell the leather of his extensive book collection, which occupies a first and second story, with the second story containing a passageway encircling the room and accessed by an oak carved circular stairway. His volumes range from the Greek classics to manuals on the breeding and care of thoroughbred horses. Few homes in the country could offer a finer library.

We are seated in the large leather sofas and overstuffed chairs that square and face the enormous fireplace. Regan attends each guest, offering hors d'oeuvres and presenting each person with their favorite drink without asking, as he already knows each guest's preference.

We all sit and talk of our activities during the day as we await our hospitable host.

Still in his riding garb and carrying his crop, Will enters the room wearing his confident, captivating smile that has served him well in business and politics throughout the years. His air of affable intelligence is evident and unspoken as he stands before us with his back to the fireplace.

"Dear friends," he begins as he accepts a drink from the ever attentive Regan. "I am so pleased that you all were able to join me in Aiken. Two years have passed since we were last together here, a time marred by a tragedy that I believe none of us will ever forget. The past eighteen months have been difficult. You all know how much Edith meant to me, and I know you share my sorrow at her passing. I will never forget all of your help and comfort on that fateful day in the preserve, and in the months that followed." His eyes search from face to face, panning the group from one end to the other. It is evident that he speaks from heartfelt sincerity.

"As you all know," Will continues, "Edith was a horsewoman of the first rank, and she loved riding in the preserve more than any other thing. I don't think she could have accepted the thought that there ever would be a time when the preserve did not exist, with all of its natural beauty and trails for horse-loving riders. As you also know, the Hitchcocks and I are co-owners of the preserve, and we have a strong relationship that I expect would ensure Edith's wish for the preserve's future, at least while we all live. And it is with this in mind that I have proposed to the Hitchcocks that the preserve be held in trust to ensure its availability for future generations. That we should do this to honor Edith's memory and ensure that our wishes remain in force beyond our lives should be the legacy that we leave, and because of the special regard I hold for each one of you, I am asking that you serve as the inaugural board of trustees upon execution of the legal document."

Murmurs of acceptance can be heard from the group as each person's gaze is fixed on Will. In return, Will's eyes shift from one guest to the other, seeking positive nods or other expressions of agreement.

"Then," he says, "if we all concur, the Hitchcocks and our attorney will be here tomorrow to finalize. We can reassemble then for the signings, and I thank you all for supporting me in this."

At that point Will holds up his hands in a motion designed to ask each guest to remain seated. "I have one other reason for executing this agreement at this time, and it is a weighty reason, with less than happy tidings," he says in a serious tone. "I have been informed by my physician that I have a physical condition that is life threatening. It is an unpredictable situation that could trigger soon or later, but inevitably it will be the cause of my demise. I have no choice but to accept these terms, face them responsibly, and ensure that my wishes reach beyond the grave," he stoically adds.

A hushed silence falls upon the group. No one moves, and even the sound of breathing cannot be heard. Everyone is transfixed as a pall falls across the room.

"And now, friends, let us repair to the reception hall, meet our fellow guests, and enjoy Mr. Casals' music," he finishes.

William C. Whitney

On January 18, 1904, Whitney was at Joye Cottage in Aiken when the Hitchcocks' home, Mons Repos, caught fire. Whitney was present at the blaze, directing the firemen and doing what he could to help. During his work that night he caught a severe cold, and after a few days returned to New York to visit his physician. After arriving in New York, his condition worsened, but that did not prevent him from attending the New York Metropolitan Opera, an organization that he helped to found. On January 28th during a performance of Parcifal, he was alone in his reserved box when his persistent illness worsened. He left before the performance was over with severe abdominal pains. The next morning, Friday, he withstood the continuing pain without calling for his physician, and it wasn't until Saturday that he instructed his secretary, Thomas Regan, to send for Dr. James. Finding a diagnosis of appendicitis, James summoned Dr. William T. Bull, a surgeon. Despite surgery to remove his appendix that evening, Whitney's condition worsened. On Tuesday Whitney's condition was grave, and his son Harry and daughter Dorothy arrived as well as his sisters, Mrs. Barney and Mrs. Dimock. Elihu Root and Whitney's brother, Henry, from Boston had also arrived. All were at his beside when he passed at four in the afternoon on February 2, 1904. He was sixty-three years of age and left an estimated fortune valued at thirty-three million dollars.

Oliver Hazard Payne

From the time of Whitney's marriage to Edith Randolph, and continuing to his death, Oliver Payne held him in contempt. He never forgave Whitney for remarrying following the death of his sister, Flora, and was the prime instigator in turning half of Whitney's family against him in his campaign of revenge and bitterness. He was successful in turning Whitney's son William (Payne) and daughter Pauline against him, and none of these attended the bedside of the dying Whitney, nor did they attend his funeral. In return, Whitney excluded William and Pauline from his will, and conversely in recompense, Oliver Payne left them both a large fortune upon his death in 1917.

Harry Payne Whitney

Upon his father's death, thirty-two-year-old Harry inherited twenty-four million dollars from his father, and became the new head of the Whitney family. His wife, Gertrude Vanderbilt Whitney, was the daughter of Cornelius and Alice Vanderbilt, and great-granddaughter of Commodore Cornelius Vanderbilt. During his lifetime he built upon the fortune left to him by his father but lacked his father's dynamism in business and politics. He shared his father's love for racehorses and maintained the family's reputation as breeders of thoroughbreds. He continued to visit Joye Cottage and Aiken throughout his life, where he raised thoroughbreds and, as a dog fancier, prize-winning dogs. He died following a short illness at his 871 Fifth Avenue New York City home from pneumonia in 1930.

Dorothy Whitney

Dorothy Whitney was seventeen years old at the time of her father's death. Her brother Harry took over the parental duties, including escorting her down the aisle in 1911 when she married Willard Straight. Dorothy was married in a very modest ceremony in Geneva, Switzerland. Straight was a poor man, and brother Harry was not pleased with Dorothy's choice of husband. While not possessing any wealth, Straight was highly successful in attaining importance in diplomatic circles as he rose through the ranks of the U.S. diplomatic corps, representing America's interests in China and Korea and attaining the post of American Consular General at Mukden. Dorothy Whitney became a widow in December of 1918 upon Willard's death in Paris from pneumonia. She was to marry again in April 1925 at the age of thirty-eight to L.K. Elmhirst of Elmhirst, Barnsley, Yorkshire, England. The marriage produced two children. Dorothy Whitney died in 1968 at the age of eighty-one.

Alexander Gunn

Alexander Gunn indeed possessed a weak heart and died of heart failure on June 15, 1901. Although he had been warned by his doctors to refrain from drinking alcoholic beverages, his bacchanalian impulses were not to be restrained. Despite failing health he continued an active lifestyle, attending the debut of his favorite niece, Helen Tracey Barney (W. Whitney's niece), attending the opera with Whitney, traveling to Aiken with Whitney, and on May 22nd of his last year, traveling with Whitney to Europe. His love of gourmet foods and Epernay champagne is thought to have caused his heart's last tremors in Zoar, Ohio.

COLONEL KUSER'S GIFT

As I drove the big black Fleetwood up Colleton Avenue, I thought about the many times I had driven my boss, Colonel Kuser, from New Jersey to his Aiken, South Carolina, home, and how many times I had checked into the Willcox Inn, where I stayed during the boss's winter visits. Like the other domestic staff, I could have stayed in the guest quarters at the colonel's home, but preferred the privacy of the Willcox, an option I enjoyed due to my status as chauffeur and personal secretary.

However, this visit to Aiken was different. There was no colonel to worry about, only myself, and indeed I did worry about myself since the doctor's diagnosis of cancer a month ago. Due to the nature of being in the colonel's employ for so many years, the opportunity to marry never surfaced, and so I was left quite alone to contemplate the growing illness within. This surely would be my last visit to Aiken.

As I drove up to the Willcox lobby entrance, I noticed the new white fluted columns that had been installed since my last visit. As usual, a prompt footman took possession of the car and directed the porter to handle the baggage. Upon entering I noticed that the foyer and lobby had been renovated, but still retained the English club atmosphere that so many patrons I knew loved and were familiar with.

"Hello, Mr. Cramer,[58] welcome back to the Willcox Inn. It's been years since we've seen you. What brings you back to Aiken?" asked Albert Willcox.

"It's so good to see you, Albert. Yes, it's been awhile, but as you may have heard, Colonel Kuser passed away on February eighth of this year,

---

58   Oscar Cramer served as personal secretary to Col. Anthony R. Kuser. He assisted Kuser with his personal and business affairs, and in April 1921, he presided over the sale of the Kuser furniture and home possessions in connection with the sale of the Kusers' Aiken winter home.

so I retired."

"Yes, I heard the news from one of our winter guests. I've taken over running the Inn since my father's passing,[59] so I'm in touch with most all of our seasonal guests now," said Albert.

"It happened at his Palm Beach estate, Los Incas," I added. "He had been ill for some time, and his personal physician, Dr. Fleming, was with him at the time of his passing. There was nothing that could be done. I thought that after so many years in his service, 1929 would be a good year to retire. So now I'm making a tour of the country, and, of course, I couldn't resist making a trip to Aiken—we have so many memories here. I hope my favorite room is available?"

"Of course it is, Oscar—available and ready! Say, why don't you dine with me this evening? My wife is visiting her sister in Chicago and I am alone. Say about seven in our dining room? You can bring me up to date on all the news from New Jersey and New York."

"It will be my pleasure, Albert. I'll see you then."

With a wave of Albert's hand, the bellman, who had anticipated the call, appeared.

"George, please take Mr. Cramer's bag to his room and see that he is comfortable."

"Yassir, Mr. Albert. Please follow me, Mr. Oscar. It's sure been a long time since we've seen y'all. I do hope y'all are well."

"Yes, George, I am well. How is your family? Please extend my best wishes to them," said I.

On the route to my room, my senses took in all the familiar smells, colors, and sounds of the Willcox. Combined, they constituted the building's personality and character developed over the space of thirty years. As we approached the stairwell leading to the upper floors' rooms, my mind's eye could still see the Lorillards and the Harrimans chatting over vintage Bordeaux in the lobby. I thought I could hear Tommy Hitchcock Jr. and his polo pals arguing technique amidst the

---

59   Frederick Willcox, founder of the Willcox Hotel, died suddenly on July 19, 1924 following a stroke.

clinking of ice against crystal. The kitchen with its gourmet smells wafting down the corridor, and through the space between the swinging doors, I could see the chef and his assistants preparing for another evening of fine dining. It was comforting to see that nothing had changed over the years.

Since I had several hours of free time before dinner, I thought that I would drive out to "Tall Pines"[60] to see what changes had taken place over the past eight years.

George brought my car around, and I could see the big grin on his face as he pulled up to the front entrance. "Mr. Oscar, that sure is a fine Cadillac Fleetwood automobile you've got there," he said as he admired the chrome trim against the deeply polished black lacquer finish.

"Yes, George, it was a generous retirement gift from the Kuser family. I've only owned it a few months, and I'm still not used to the attention it draws wherever I go."

It was a short ride from Colleton Avenue to Tall Pines, and as I turned into the semicircular entrance, I could see a lady who I thought resembled Mrs. Hofmann[61] at the front door, engaged in a passing conversation with several young women, obviously students, who were dressed in velvet green riding jackets, helmets in hand, and leading their mounts to the school's stable. It reminded me that school would soon be out, as spring was upon us, and many of these young riders would be returning to the north with their families. The many dogwoods, azaleas, and hydrangeas planted by Mrs. Kuser were in bloom, and the home looked delightful in its frame of pinks, whites, blues, and reds from these marvelous plants. Of course, the colonel also took an active interest in the plantings around Tall Pines, planting oak and tree specimens particularly attractive for bird nesting.

As a naturalist with a very serious interest in ornithology, his gardening influence could still be seen everywhere around the property.

60   "Tall Pines" was Col. Kuser's winter cottage, located at 840 Whiskey Road.
61   Marie Eustis Hofmann founded the Fermata School for Girls in her Laurens Street home in 1919. In 1921, she purchased the Kuser winter cottage and moved the school to that location.

I remembered 1909, when he financed the Kuser-Beebe expedition to study birds in Ceylon, India, Burma, the Malay States, Java, Borneo, China, and Japan. The findings of that expedition were still taught today.

"Hello, are you Mrs. Hofmann?" I asked.

"Why, yes, and I believe you're Mr. Cramer, aren't you? You were personal secretary to Colonel Kuser when we purchased his home for the school," Marie said tentatively.

"Yes, that's right. I hope that everything is going well for the school and you," I said.

"Oh yes, the school is prospering. Each year we have seen an increase in our enrollment, and thanks to our staff we've expanded our curriculum each year as well. By my own desire, my role here has been greatly reduced as I spend much of my time in Bar Harbor[62] or Europe. I'm here this year only for graduation, which comes up in a few weeks. You see, Josef[63] and I divorced a couple of years ago, and since then I have lost many interests—too many memories to deal with," said Marie in a trailing, subdued voice.

"I'm sorry to hear that. Well, perhaps now is a bad time and I shouldn't intrude. I thought I would try to visit the colonel's home one last time, but…"

"Oh, you're not intruding and it's no problem to come in and visit. The colonel has done so much for Aiken, especially with the hospital,[64] and I know you were a great help to him in getting those things done. Join me, and we'll both tour the home again," said Marie, now with a bit more optimism in her voice.

As we entered through the foyer, I could see the library, where the colonel spent so much time with his favorite books, three hundred of

---

62   The Hofmanns maintained homes in Bar Harbor, Maine; Switzerland, and Laurens St., Aiken.

63   Josef Hofmann, internationally acclaimed pianist, was married to Marie Eustis 1905–1927.

64   A. R. Kuser played an important fund-raising role in the winter colony's initiative to build Aiken's first hospital. He served on the hospital's founding board of directors following its opening in May 1917.

which were donated to the Aiken library when the home was sold.

"I see the library is still being used for its original purpose," said I.

"Yes, Mr. Cramer, and if the imported floor rugs, the Turkish silk hanging rug, the old china, and the teakwood living room set were still here, you probably wouldn't know Colonel Kuser had left," said Marie as she waved her arm before the well-appointed rooms.

"Yes, I remember the day we sold many of the family's personal items. There was just too much to transport back to New Jersey, so they had to be sold. As I remember, Mrs. Massengale and Messrs. Terry and Miller bought most of them, the bedsteads, chairs, sideboards, and china cabinets. I see you've kept the draperies and the wall hangings; they seem like old friends," I said as I privately reminisced about pleasant winter stays.

Our tour of the home was cut short when Mrs. Mary Curtis Bok, a Fermata school board member, suddenly appeared from the rear of the home and called Mrs. Hofmann away on a matter of what I assumed was administrative urgency, judging from the look on her face.

"I can find my way out," I said. "Thank you for your time, and good luck with Fermata, Mrs. Hofmann." I turned to leave.

I drove down Whiskey Road with memories of past Aiken winters swirling through my mind. Many of those memories were of a vicarious nature, since my role was one of support for whatever the colonel was involved in; whether it was golf at the Palmetto Club, or being out at Whitney Field, or his bird-watching forays into Hitchcock woods, or providing the clerical and administrative services for his many philanthropic endeavors.

Since it was still early and I had time to spare before meeting Albert for dinner, I decided to drive through town and see what changes had taken place. I thought about my forty years of employment with the Kuser family.

My life with the Kusers began in 1889 and continued until the colonel's passing on February 8, 1929. As a native of Trenton, New Jersey,

I knew of Colonel Kuser, who had been a resident of the city since his family moved there from Newark when he was a five-year-old child. I knew of him because of his prominence in state government, serving on the staffs of three New Jersey governors: Leon Abbett (1884–1887 & 1890–1893),[65] George T. Werts (1893–1896), and John W. Griggs (1896–1898).[66]

Although he never served in the military, he was given the title of colonel while serving on the personal staff of Governor Abbett. Later governors also appointed him to various boards and commissions that had oversight of state public utilities, public service commission, and state highway and transportation departments. And it was during those years, through his political affiliations, that he met John Fairfield Dryden and fell in love with his daughter, Susie, who he married at Trenton on December 1, 1896. The Kusers had two children: John Dryden, born in 1897, who became a senator in the State of New Jersey, and Cynthia, born in 1910, who as a rebellious child and adolescent went on to a life of intrigue and promiscuity.

Becoming a member of the Dryden family through marriage had tremendous financial, political, and social ramifications, as John Fairfield Dryden was the founder of The Prudential Insurance Company. He was also a Republican. His business interests included street railways, banks, and other financial interests in New Jersey, New York, and Pennsylvania. The colonel's early political appointments came from staunch Democratic governors, until John Griggs was elected, a Republican, and the colonel was by that time transitioned and firmly traveling in his father-in-law's Republican political orbit. In 1902, Dryden was elected as a Republican to the U.S. Senate to fill the vacancy caused by the death of Senator William J. Sewell. He served one term, which ended in 1907. John Dryden lived for four more years

---

65 Abbett was appointed judge on N.J. Supreme Court in 1893. He died in 1894 of diabetes complications.

66 Griggs stepped down from the governorship to accept appointment by Pres. McKinley to the office of U.S. Attorney General and served in that capacity until 1901.

and passed on November 24, 1911 at the age of seventy-two from pneumonia following the removal of gallstones. His estate was valued at fifty million dollars, and the colonel's wife, Susie, was Dryden's only child.

As I drove around town and passed by the Hitchcock/Whitney wooded preserve, with its trails and fresh country scent, I was reminded why the Kusers were drawn to Aiken. With the pines and hardwoods flourishing, the dogwoods in bloom, I could almost hear and envision the distant sound of riders mounted and galloping down the many paths. The Kusers' love of nature and land preservation, along with the colonel's love of horses and hounds made Aiken the perfect place to while away the harsh New Jersey winters.

I headed further downtown, passing the old Thestone Theatre, which brought back a specific memory of one of the colonel's many philanthropic efforts. It was here on March 10, 1917 that through the colonel's business connections, William Fox's million-dollar picture, *A Daughter of the Gods*, an elaborate underwater fantasy following a Wagnerian mythological theme,[67] was shown, with all the proceeds being donated to the Aiken Hospital Fund.

It was the colonel who became the original chief financier of William Fox's dream to form the Fox Film Corporation[68] in 1915. With the colonel's $200,000 investment, Vilmos Fried, better known as William Fox after his emigration to the U.S. from Hungary, became an innovator in movie production and was known for his epic movies, employing large casts and grandiose sets. As a major stockholder, Colonel Kuser was an important board member of Fox's new company. *A Daughter of the Gods* did have a one-million-dollar budget, the largest of any movie ever produced. As I reminisced about this, Mr. Fox was busy buying the Loew family's holdings in MGM. If he was successful, his would be the largest movie production company in the country.[69]

---

67   Many compared it to the story line of Wagner's opera *Das Rheingold*.
68   Today the business is known as The Fox Broadcasting Co., and 20th Century Fox.
69   MGM boss Louis B. Mayer, upon learning of Fox's scheme, used his considerable political clout to

A Daughter of the Gods was the most elaborate movie of its day, using a full orchestra and featuring the noted Australian silent star Annette Kellerman, an actress of rare beauty. A film of this scope would have been reserved for the large markets in New York, Philadelphia, Los Angeles, and Atlanta. Such a film would never have been shown in Aiken without the colonel's involvement. Moreover, Colonel Kuser persuaded Mr. Fox to forbid the movie's showing anywhere within one hundred miles of Aiken, thereby ensuring a large turnout and a greater financial take for the Aiken Hospital Fund. This wasn't the first time that the colonel used his business connections to help the city of Aiken, I remembered. In 1915, he was instrumental in securing James Barnes and his moving pictures, *Through Central Africa from Coast to Coast*, for the Aiken Theatre, and the proceeds of the performance, $1,020, went to the Aiken Relief Society.

I noticed that it was getting late, and I needed to head back to the Willcox to allow enough time to freshen up and prepare for dinner with Albert.

As I entered the Willcox dining room, I could see the same finely carved and brocade-accented chairs, and the claw-footed, mahogany tables covered with fine white linen. One would think that the room was set for a very special occasion, with shining Sterling and sparkling Waterford, and a fresh bouquet of blue hydrangea at every table. Anywhere else it would have been special, but of course, this was de rigueur for the Willcox Inn. I noticed Albert in the far corner at a small table for two, waving me on, and I began heading in that direction. As I made my way, I saw a number of familiar faces—C. Oliver and Hope Iselin were dining with the Goodyears, the Holley family were at the front table, and Mrs. McLean with her son, who was a student at Aiken Preparatory School, occupied a table nearest a window overlooking the rose-covered trellis on the outside patio. I nodded good evening as I

---

persuade the Justice Department to sue Fox for violating the federal antitrust law. This, combined with a serious automobile accident Fox was involved in and the stock market crash of Oct. 1929, foiled his plans to obtain a controlling interest in MGM.

passed, and nodding smiles were returned, even though some may only have faint memory of where they had seen me before. We were close to the end of the season, and perhaps they all were enjoying a last dinner at the Willcox before heading back north.

When I reached his table, Albert, ever the perfect host, rose to shake my hand. "Oscar, it is so good you could join me. I've taken the liberty of ordering the Bordeaux; still your favorite, I hope?"

"Thank you, yes, you know how some things never change for me," I replied. "Albert, you've done a marvelous job in renovating the Inn. I love the colonial architecture facade with the Southern flair."

"Yes, our clientele continues to grow every winter and spring, so we decided to add another floor, renovate the central hall, and replace it with an expanded foyer and lobby. We completed the work last October, just in time for the season. And now we've petitioned the city for permission to widen Colleton Avenue and create a small park to relieve the arrival and departure congestion that inevitably happens every year. I hope to have that completed before next season.

"So tell me, Oscar, what news is there of the Kuser family? I heard a story some years ago, not long after the colonel left Aiken, about a mysterious burglary that took place at his family's villa in Bernardsville."

"Albert, it was the most peculiar event that ever happened during all the years I've worked for the Kuser family," said I. "As I remember, it happened in the early morning hours of November first, 1921. There were eighteen people asleep in the home that night, including the colonel's wife, Susie, their eleven-year-old daughter, Cynthia, his son, John Dryden, and his daughter-in-law, Brooke. Brooke's mother, Mrs. John R. Russell, in addition to security and domestic staff, were also there. The colonel always insisted that his children, including John Dryden, who had been married for two years, continue to live in his home.[70] The incident began around two a.m. when the butler's wife,

---

70   Anthony Kuser, while a good-hearted philanthropist, was punctual, domineering, and reportedly always needed to be in control.

Mrs. Brewsher, thought she heard a shot. Mrs. Russell, who also heard a noise, thought she heard the vibration of a large drill. The night watchman, Mr. Alexander Hill, spent the night awake in the telephone room located directly beneath the only window, one that was heavily screened, where a thief could gain access to the colonel's bedroom, yet $20,000 in jewels were taken from a locked and bolted room where they were stored. The colonel stated that he felt something touch the bridge of his nose in the middle of the night, and later awakened at 4:30 a.m. with a severe headache. Later, he learned that the same had happened to Mrs. Kuser in her bedroom, as well as to other family members. It was theorized that the thief or thieves had chloroformed the family members while they slept, then went about the marble-floored rooms with elaborate wooden panels finished with gold leaf, searching for valuables. The colonel's son, John Dryden, and his wife occupied the apartment on the next floor above the colonel's, some twenty-five feet higher. Access there was very limited and blocked by bolted doors. Despite this limited access, the colonel's daughter-in-law, Brooke, had her engagement ring slipped from her finger as she was drugged. In all, forty articles of jewelry were stolen as well as some cash. The thieves left no exit trail, and there was no evidence that there was ever a break-in. The colonel, as well as the Preferred Accident Insurance Company, put up a $5,000 reward for the capture of the thief or thieves, but no one was ever arrested for the crime."

Albert's face was transfixed in consternation throughout my recitation, and I wondered if he really believed this could have happened as described, but it did. As the waiter began serving our hors d'oeuvres, Albert continued the conversation. "Well, what of the family now, since the colonel's recent death? How are they coping?"

"Things are not well at all, Albert," I said as I began another, much sadder story of this prominent family. "While still in the car, following the completion of cemetery services, Dryden and Brooke announced their divorce. For the colonel's sake they stayed together, but never have

I seen a greater mismatch or abusive situation.

"If my memory serves correctly, John Dryden Kuser married Roberta Brooke Russell in April 1919 at St. John's Episcopal Church. Brooke, as she is called, is the daughter of Colonel John Russell, who is commandant of the U.S. Marine Corps. Of course, marrying the grandson of the late senator, and founder of Prudential Insurance Company, John F. Dryden opened a whole new political world for her. And, with a father-in-law who shared in a fifty-million-dollar inheritance, a whole new lifestyle awaited. She was only seventeen at the time of the marriage and, as we learned, totally unprepared for Dryden's[71] appetites and abusive temperament, beginning with the first night of their honeymoon at Green Briar in West Virginia. Although she had lived in many states and foreign countries as a result of her father's military transfers, she was naïve about sex and her new husband's philandering tendencies and propensity for overindulgence in alcoholic beverages. In any case the couple moved into Colonel Kuser's mansion, Faircourt, which sprawled over 250 acres in Bernardsville, New Jersey.

"In 1924, a son was born to them, and he was named Tony Dryden in honor of his paternal grandfather and great-grandfather. Through his father's connections, Dryden became employed by several different businesses, but was not very successful in any. His upbringing and lifestyle were such that he was unable to focus on business details. As it developed, his talents seemed to be in the political arena, which enabled him to be elected New Jersey State Senator, but his political career was lackluster and devoid of any meaningful legislation.

"The home life continued to be antagonistic, even more so after moving into their own home. It was strongly suspected that Brooke had become a battered wife, although she was silent about much of what went on at home. One story circulated that Dryden had struck and broken Brooke's jaw during her pregnancy. But it was undeniable what took place in public, when Dryden would embarrass her verbally

---

71   John was always called by his middle name, his maternal grandfather's last name.

at social events. At the time of announcing their divorce, Dryden was already having an affair with a married woman, a Vieva Fisher Banks, who had three daughters. As it turns out, Brooke was also involved with a married stock broker, Buddie Marshall, a Yale graduate whom she had met at a fox hunt," I said. "So, the colonel's death brought to surface all the animosities and simmering anger within his family. The smoldering enmity that lurked in his home was now a fire loosed, and making up for time lost during its years of suppression. As far as I can remember, it was only a few winters that Dryden and Brooke came to Tall Pines on Whiskey Road. Although Brooke enjoyed horsemanship and the fox hunt, their interests were not consistent with those of Colonel Anthony Kuser.

"The colonel's other child, his daughter Cynthia, who was born in 1910, has always been a rebellious child, and I fear for her future. Sorry for that sad news, Albert, but things don't always turn out the way one wants them to. I know that that's not what the colonel ever wanted," I observed.

"You're right, Oscar, but the colonel's memory here in Aiken will always be one filled with appreciation for his generosity and philanthropic activities on behalf of the community."

At this point I reached into the inside pocket of my jacket and withdrew a white envelope. "Albert, may I leave this envelope with you, and would you promise to pass it along to Mrs. Hofmann at the Fermata School?"

"Certainly, Oscar, you can count on me to pass it to her very soon."

"Thank you. The colonel and I appreciate it. The last thing he did before passing on was to hand me this envelope and to be sure it was received by the Fermata School. I don't know if I will ever be back in Aiken, and wanted to be sure of its delivery."

"No problem, Oscar, I'll take care of it. Now, check out our new dinner menu. I think you'll find some great selections…"

The Envelope delivered by Oscar Cramer contained a check payable to the Fermata School for Girls in the amount of $500,000. It was accompanied by a terse note addressed to Marie Hofmann. *"I wish to make this gift anonymously, and indeed I ask that no publicity be attached to your receipt of the enclosed. Please take good care of my home."* Signed, Col. Anthony R. Kuser.

Anthony R. Kuser was the son of Austrian-German immigrants. He began as a pants presser, was successful as a wholesale dealer for a brewery, went on to serve on the staffs of several New Jersey governors, and from that association married into tremendous wealth and power. His wife Susie's inheritance provided the main base of his wealth. Following their marriage, Susie became anonymous, invisible to the public eye, with little to no public references about her life and activities. Kuser served as president of the South Jersey Gas and Electric Lighting Company; however, his lasting mark will always be in the area of philanthropy, including notable activity in his adopted winter home, Aiken. His involvement in establishing the Aiken Hospital was substantial in his personal generosity and fund-raising efforts. At the reception introducing the new hospital to the community, some 168 Aiken citizens endorsed a note of thanks as published by *The Journal and Review* of May 23, 1917. The front page article noted, "A card of thanks to the donors was drawn up and those present signed it. It reads as follows: The undersigned citizens of Aiken desire to express their deep appreciation and gratitude to Mr. and Mrs. C. Oliver Iselin, Mr. W.K. Vanderbilt, and Col. A.R. Kuser for the establishment of the Aiken Hospital. It is felt that the donors' munificence will operate for the lasting good of this community, and will fill a long existing need."

Colonel Kuser was also instrumental in the building of the second clubhouse at Palmetto Golf Club in 1902.

John Dryden Kuser, Colonel Kuser's eldest child, led a life marked by privilege and indulgence. His relationship with his first wife, Brooke Russell Kuser, was tempestuous and abusive. It was only through his father's influence that he was able to land substantial employment with several manufacturers, and was unsuccessful with all. Dryden launched his political career in 1922 at age twenty-five, held several locally elected offices, and won a New Jersey Senate seat in 1929. His profligate lifestyle would eventually put an end to his political career. He had been described by a family member as fast drinking and fast smoking; he enjoyed fast women and possessed an incredibly calculating, quick, brilliant mind. He was unable to make fortunes like his father, but was great at spending them. His political career came to an end in 1935, when his second wife divorced him amid accusations of abuse and cruelty. In all, he was married four times before his death in 1964, at the age of sixty-six.

Cynthia Kuser, Colonel Kuser's second child, led a life outside the norm, a life that many would find strange, or the fodder of spy novels. As an adolescent, her rebelliousness was noted. As a young woman, she developed a reputation for being fast, beautiful, and unprincipled. One newspaper source noted that her lovers included the mobster Lucky Luciano, the Spanish matador Manolete, and Alfred Sloan, the head of General Motors—all while she was married to her first husband, Theodore Herbst. Later, during her sham marriage to Arthur Earle, she began an ongoing, lifelong affair with the Russian defector Victor Kravchenko, one of the most influential and earliest defectors to the U.S. from the Soviet Union. Their relationship was kept secret, even to her two sons, Andrew and Tony, whose paternity was with Kravchenko. It was not until 1965, shortly following Kravchenko's death, that the boys learned the truth about their paternal origins.

Kravchenko gained praise with his book *I Chose Freedom*, which became renowned and was considered a forerunner to Solzhenitsyn's *Gulag Archipelago*, recounting the atrocities of the Soviet system. Because of this, Kravchenko was targeted by the Soviet KGB, and to protect Cynthia and sons, their relationship was kept secret. In retaliation for his defection and his written disclosures, Kravchenko's parents and other family members who remained in the Soviet Union had already been murdered by the Soviet secret police. Kravchenko was found dead in his Manhattan apartment in 1965 with a single gunshot to the head. Cynthia Kuser Earle died in 1985 at the age of seventy-five.

Brooke Russell Kuser, Colonel Kuser's daughter-in-law, produced one child, Tony, in 1924 with her first husband, Dryden. A few years after her 1929 divorce from him, she married her lover, Buddie Marshall, to whom she was married for twenty years, until his death in 1952. In 1953, she married the misanthropic, multi-millionaire Vincent Astor,[72] and through that marriage she became the leading socialite in the rarified world of high society. The love of her life was Buddie Marshall; however, in a bereaved panic following his death, she, within one year, married not for love, but security. She was Mrs. Vincent Astor for five and a half years until his death. Only after Astor's death did she develop the image of the Mrs. Astor that the public and society would come to know. As Mrs. Astor, and head of the Vincent Astor Foundation, she gave away $200 million to New York charities and institutions. Her tumultuous years as Mrs. Dryden Kuser were long past, not forgotten, and never dwelt upon. In her later years, Brooke Astor was energetic, vibrant, and kept a full-time secretary busy recording her ongoing appointments, society gatherings, board and civic meetings. She continued to circulate, by the season, between Europe and her homes: Cove End, Northeast Harbor, Maine; Holly Hill, Briarcliff Manor, New York; and Manhattan. However, by 2003, she was forgetful and was in the developing stages of Alzheimer's disease. Mrs. Brooke Astor

---

72   Eldest son of John Jacob Astor IV, the *Titanic* disaster victim

passed away at age 105 in her Westchester country home, Holly Hill, on August 13, 2007, of pneumonia. She was interred in Sleepy Hollow Cemetery, Sleepy Hollow, New York. Shortly before her death, her only son by Dryden Kuser, Anthony Marshall,[73] was removed from guardianship of his mother, due to alleged neglect and abuse. In 2009, he went to trial on charges of grand larceny, criminal possession of stolen property, forgery, and several other charges.

Following her divorce from Dryden Kuser, Brooke never returned to Aiken as far as is known.

---

73   Anthony Kuser so identified with Buddie Marshall that he changed his name from Kuser to Marshall during his mother's second marriage.

WILLIAM K. VANDERBILT'S AIKEN LEGACY

March 15, 1877

On Thursday morning the sound of hammers and saws could be heard on the Aiken courthouse grounds as the gallows' frame was being completed. Carpenters had been working for the past two days to make ready for the next day's executions. Some were crafting the trapdoor and others filling the counterweight sandbags that would be suspended under the platform. Their goal was to be finished with the steps and gibbet by noon so there would be plenty of time for testing the ropes and trapdoor release.

Time was growing short for the five black men[74] who sat in their irons in Aiken's courthouse jail, well within earshot of the pounding hammers and the saw's biting hum. They knew well that they were the object of the carpenters' buzz, and that on the morrow between 10 a.m. and 2 p.m. they would each be led up the scaffold steps—hooded, hands and feet bound—and experience the feel of a horsehair rope tightened around their necks before their last moments on earth. With anxious misery they watched the construction bustle through the bars, which was also watched from the outside by ten armed citizen-guard volunteers strategically posted around the jail perimeter. The volunteers were there to prevent another attempted escape, for two weeks prior, with the aid of outside confederates, the prisoners had almost succeeded in breaking out.

The jail was an add-on to the property, an outbuilding detached

---

74   Lucius Thomas, John Henry Dennis, Steve Anderson, Nelson Brown, and one unnamed

from the courthouse. And on the very ground where the gallows were being erected once stood a beautiful rose arch that produced the most beautiful roses each spring. The courthouse itself was once called the Gregg mansion, named after its first owner, William Gregg, who constructed the thirty-room mansion for his son in 1832[75] before the railroad came to Aiken. Gregg owned a large tract of land around the lot where he built the home on the corner of Colleton Avenue and Union Street, an area that was to become the heart of the city of Aiken with the coming of the railroad in 1833.

In 1871, South Carolina's newest county, Aiken County, was cobbled together by the state legislature using parts of five existing abutting counties, which necessitated that a jail and courthouse be built or bought. After study, an appointed commission recommended that the Gregg mansion be bought and converted to the Aiken County courthouse. The home was bought for $19,400 and it served as the seat of justice for Aiken County until 1881.

The five desperate black men who now awaited their executions had been convicted of the recent murder of two German immigrant farmers named Hausmann and Pothman, which took place on their farm near Banks Mill. It was theorized that the motive was robbery, and upon resisting, both men were killed by the five assailants. After due investigation the sheriff and his deputies arrested the suspects. And although they professed their innocence, all were convicted after deliberation by the jury, and sentenced to death by hanging.

This night would pass slowly while each restless man wrestled with his thoughts and emotions and fought his nerves. The citizen-volunteer guards outside could hear the occasional sound of low, dull clank of chain against iron coming through the bars, as each man, seeking comfort, moved about within his limited space. All had refused a last meal, and although it was perceived as one final act of defiance, the reality

---

75 Some sources place the building of the home in 1855. *The Aiken Standard* has reported its construction between 1832 and 1834.

of knotted stomachs being squeezed beyond control by nerves as men face certain death perhaps had more to do with the decision to abstain.

March 16, 1877

At seven o'clock the first light of impending spring began to break in the east. None of the prisoners had slept. A preacher, accompanied by the jailer, came to the cell to offer final spiritual comfort. He was refused and sent away.

The jailer, who had been within earshot of the prisoners' cell that morning, overheard the five men discuss a postmortem pact, a strange agreement that would not be credible to most rational people. They agreed that if it were any way possible following their death, their spirits would rejoin, return to occupy the courthouse grounds, and lay claim to the space forever. The jailer disregarded the conversation and attributed it to the inventive gibberish of five illiterate Negroes.

At nine forty-five it was almost time to begin, and all was ready. A morbidly curious crowd had gathered on Colleton Avenue, but they were kept at a distance by the extra deputies who had been summoned to control such traffic. The citizen-volunteer guards were still at their posts, and two accompanied the sheriff into the jail to retrieve the first prisoner.

A hooded executioner stood on the platform, along with a preacher who held a bible in hand and the local magistrate, who would read the sentence and direct the executioner at the appointed time.

At the cell the sheriff called out the first prisoner, Lucius Thomas. Led from the jail still in his chains, he stepped out into the yard. With eyes squinting as they adjusted from the cell's dimness, his large frame slowly plodded to the scaffold steps with each footfall sounding the clink, clank of chain against iron. Although it was cool that morning, beads of sweat formed on the prisoner's brow. The stink of sweat and urine radiated from his soiled prison clothes. Once atop the platform, the sheriff guided him to a spot above the trapdoor as the deputies substituted his shackles for rope. The preacher was now reading from his bible in a low, subdued voice. The magistrate began to read from the execution order:

"Lucius Thomas, you have been found guilty of murder in the first degree by a lawful jury, and in accordance with this lawful execution order, you are sentenced to hang until dead."

The prisoner was then asked if he had anything to say.

The prisoner's eyes had been downcast for the entire time he was led to the scaffold and tied with the rope. He now looked up with determined, piercing eyes directed at the gathered crowd. His lips trembled as he struggled to gain control of his nerves. Through black, rotted teeth and in a low, gravelly voice, he spat out four words. "I will be back."

The magistrate nodded to the masked executioner, who placed the black hood over the prisoner's head. The horsehair rope was tightened around his neck, and he began to shake uncontrollably as he lost control of his nerves; urine could be seen streaming from a pant leg. A second nod from the magistrate and the executioner pulled the lever actuating the trapdoor. The squeaking hinge and the clunk of the heavy wooden trapdoor, the violent strain of rope from the pull, and then a snap as the man dropped with legs kicking, and then twitching, then still. It was over in less than a minute.

And so it happened again, and again, with each taking their turn until all five had met the court's justice on March 16, 1877.

The Aiken County Courthouse vacated the Gregg mansion at 306 Colleton Avenue for a new facility in 1881. At that time the county government sold the property to Otis Chafee, whose home on Kalmia Hill had recently burned. Chafee demolished the jail outbuilding and returned the main property to its original splendor, including the large rose arch in the side yard where the gallows once stood. His extensive renovations returned the home to its original design when first built by Gregg. Following his death the home passed through inheritance to Emma Chafee Walpole, who later sold it to winter colonist Joseph Harriman, a member of the wealthy investment banking and insurance interest family.

In 1903, William K. Vanderbilt, great-grandson of railroad baron Commodore Cornelius Vanderbilt, married Anne Harriman Sands, his second wife and daughter of banker Oliver Harriman. William loved thoroughbreds and Anne was an avid horsewoman, and the Vanderbilts had close friendship ties with a number of Aiken winter colonists who shared their avocation. In 1914, they acquired the Gregg mansion from family member Joseph Harriman and continued to be winter visitors until William's death in July 1920. Following William's death, the home was passed as part of the estate to sons Willie Jr. and Harold, and daughter Consuelo,[76] who was now living in England as the Duchess of Marlboro.

March 16, 1921

It had been nearly a year since their father's death, upon which the three siblings took possession of 306 Colleton Avenue through inheritance. This rare gathering in Aiken was prompted by Consuelo's upcoming second marriage[77] on July 4th to Lieutenant Colonel Louis Jacques Balsan of the French army. It would be a last opportunity to gather together before Consuelo's permanent removal to France. At present she was en route to New York from South Hampton aboard the Berengaria. From there she would take the Vanderbilt's private Pullman south to Aiken for the reunion.

It was evident that spring arrived early to Aiken in 1921, with

---

76   Consuelo, William's eldest child, at one time was secretly engaged to Winthrop Rutherfurd, but was pressured into marrying Charles Richard John Spencer Churchill, Duke of Marlborough, by her socially ambitious mother, Alva. Essentially broke except for a title, the duke's matrimonial motivation was a need for Vanderbilt money to maintain his lifestyle at Blenheim Castle.

77   Still in her twenties, she separated from Marlborough in 1906 and had the marriage annulled after eleven unhappy years.

the purple redbuds, pink and white dogwoods, and red azaleas on the Vanderbilt property either in bloom or starting to bloom. And on the side yard stood a large bloodred rose arch filled with new blossoms that, for some inexplicable reason, always seemed to bloom in March, rather early for roses. Either side of the crushed stone drive leading up to the Vanderbilt cottage was bordered by a low hedge accented by two blooming pink dogwoods located about midway between the street and the home's façade. The drive divided and curved into a semicircle before reaching the front piazza, forming a roundabout dominated by palmetto palms surrounded by hedge, which formed the center. The Vanderbilts called their winter retreat "Elm Court."[78]

Taking a rare vacation from the railroad business, Harold had been at the home for about a month, and now awaited the arrival of his brother Willie Jr., and the next day, his sister Consuelo.

Harold was thirty-seven years old in 1921. He was the youngest child and second son of William K. and Alva Vanderbilt. Harold had a privileged upbringing and was a graduate of Harvard College and Harvard Law School, where he graduated in 1910. Following graduation he took his place in senior management of the family's railroad companies. His passions were yacht racing and card games. He is known for his innovations in the game of bridge, namely Contract Bridge, which was Harold's invention. He also had a keen interest in Vanderbilt University's welfare and served on the University's Board of Trust as president for many years.

Upon hearing the crunch of tires displacing crushed stone and two quick horn blasts, Harold was alerted to look out the upstairs bedroom window to see the big, powerful Mercedes come up the drive with his older brother, Willie Jr., behind the wheel.

Bounding down the staircase and out the door, Harold reached the piazza about the same time as Willie was reaching the front step.

---

78   The winter home was named after the Vanderbilt summer home located in the Berkshires, Lenox, Massachusetts, which was built by family member Emily Vanderbilt, granddaughter of the commodore, and her husband, William D. Sloane.

"Dear brother Willie, how have you been and how was the trip south? I wasn't expecting you until tomorrow," said Harold.

"The trip was fine. I may have set a New York to Aiken speed record with my new Mercedes, Mike.[79] It's the latest from Germany and I just received her off the dock a week ago."

"Yes, I know your penchant for fast cars. You're the only one in our family who would drive such a distance. Consuelo will be here tomorrow. She'll be coming in on Father's Pullman, arriving at the Aiken depot in late afternoon. Come in, relax, let's have a drink, and bring me up to date on New York and the latest news of Mother's social cause adventures," said Harold, clearly excited about his brother's arrival.

"Okay, Mike, just give me a minute to refresh and unpack. I hope my old room upstairs is still available? I'll be down and ready for a drink in a few minutes; the last two hundred miles were grueling," returned Willie.

Willie Vanderbilt Jr. was born on March 2, 1878, and was known as "Willie K" until his father died, whence he became William Jr. Unlike his younger brother, he never finished Harvard and dropped out after his first year. His pampered lifestyle allowed him to visit Europe early and frequently. It was there, in France, that he first gained a fascination with automobiles and was introduced to auto racing. He enjoyed yachting and horse racing, but his first love was autos and auto racing. At that time France and Germany were far ahead of the Americans when it came to automotive innovation and grand prix style racing. Willie had tried to introduce that racing format in the U.S., but his proposals were coldly received and rejected by many local governments. After all, the automobile was a passing fancy, and only served to endanger horse-drawn vehicles, farm animals wandering onto the roadway, and unwary pedestrians. However, he did achieve some success in 1910 when he proposed building the Long Island Motor Parkway, which would be reserved for motor cars only. This event came about following

---

79   Harold was known as "Mike" within the family and among close friends.

numerous accidents involving animals, pedestrians, repeated speeding arrests, and other driving mishaps. At that time Willie was president of the infant American Automobile Association, which, along with being a Vanderbilt, carried some influence in gaining the necessary approvals from local authorities. Of course, the idea also budding in his mind was that this same parkway would be used as a course for an annual race, attracting drivers worldwide. Indeed, Willie ultimately had his way, and the annual race he founded would gain national and international attention as the "Vanderbilt Cup."

Although his temperament wasn't attuned to executive corporate life, Willie did spend time learning the management rigors of the New York Central Railroad. He continued to work until his father's death in 1920, whereupon he felt a sort of manumission from this disciplined lifestyle, and began to live the life that would make him most happy. After all, he had just inherited twenty-four million dollars.

Since the summer of 1899, Willie had been married to Virginia Fair. Virginia, or "Birdie" as she was known, was the daughter of James Fair, who achieved great wealth through his "Comstock Lode," one of the largest silver mine strikes ever in Nevada. At the time of her wedding, Virginia had already inherited and controlled her father's estate since his passing in 1894. Additionally, Virginia had ties with the Oelrichs family through her sister's marriage. The Oelrichs controlled the trans-Atlantic shipping line Norddeutsche Lloyd. It was quite apparent to the Vanderbilts that they now had an opportunity to link their railroads with cargo shipments coming into New York Harbor.

The marriage produced three children: Muriel, born in 1904, Consuelo, born in 1905, and a son, William Kissam III, born in 1907. The marriage did not progress well, however, and by the spring of 1908, Willie and Virginia were living apart with no plans to divorce, as Virginia was a devout Catholic. Included in the reasons for the split was Willie's wild spending, which Virginia considered a squandering of her inheritance. At the time, Willie was still living on an annual allowance provided by his father, a stipend he always exceeded, leaving her inheritance as the only other source of funds to pick up the shortfall and maintain their lifestyle.

When Willie came downstairs and entered the kitchen, his brother had already poured him a gin and tonic, one of his favorite relaxation beverages. They hadn't seen one another since their father's funeral, and Harold was clearly delighted to see his brother again.

"Well, Willie, what are you going to do with your twenty-four million?" asked Harold playfully.

"Father had always said that money can't buy happiness, and I now know how right he was. As you know, Virginia and I have been apart for some twelve years now, and the only contact we have is through the children. My diversions with racing, auto cars, and travel are just that. While I enjoy it all, they do not replace having meaningful relationships. They serve as a pleasant anesthetic to the ways of the world," said Willie reflectively.

"You know, Willie, when Consuelo arrives, we need to discuss what we will do with this property. While we've always enjoyed Aiken in the winter, it was Father's and Anne's love of thoroughbreds and polo that motivated the purchase of this home. And neither Consuelo, you, or I share that same avocation to the extent that they did," observed Harold.

"I'm all for selling as soon as possible, and I'm fairly certain that with Consuelo's move to France after the wedding, she will probably agree with that course of action. However, I will miss seeing Harry Payne[80] here each winter. Perhaps we shouldn't sell too quickly," said Willie, after second thoughts.

"As you know, Father was a practical but sentimental man all his

---

80   Harry Payne Whitney, son of William C. Whitney and heir to Joye Cottage on Easy Street, and Willie were close friends. At one point the two had motored across Italy, Sicily, North Africa, and France on a bachelor adventure that lasted for months.

life, and given our lifestyles I don't think he would mind if we sell the place. After all, he did buy it for Anne, and why not? She was the love of his life. He would have done anything for her, or for us, for that matter. Do you not miss him, Willie?" asked Harold as the two pondered their now nearly empty glasses of gin.

William Kissam Vanderbilt, father of Willie Jr., Harold, and Consuelo, had become the head of the Vanderbilt clan with the death of his older brother, Cornelius, in September 1899. Up until that time, he and his brother had shared control and management[81] of the family railroads since the death of their father, William Henry, in 1885. Although management was shared by the brothers, it was clear that Cornelius had the greater role in operating the business. However, once William was head of the family, he also took the helm of the New York Central and the other railroads controlled by the Vanderbilt family.

William Kissam Vanderbilt was born on December 12, 1849, the second son of William H. "Billy" Vanderbilt, and grandson of "Commodore" Cornelius Vanderbilt.

In April of 1875, at the age of twenty-six, William married his first wife, Alva Erskine Smith, who came from a well-to-do Alabama family. Alva was an aggressive woman with social ambitions that would drive most of her actions throughout her marriage to Vanderbilt. To that end and within two years of the marriage, Alva commissioned the building of their new home at 660 Fifth Avenue,[82] New York, which resembled a French Renaissance chateau. This was followed in 1878 by her new, Queen Anne style retreat on Long Island, named "Idle Hour."[83] Still, this was to be followed by the most opulent of all the homes, at Newport, Rhode Island, where she built "Marble House" to commemorate her thirty-ninth birthday.

---

81   Cornelius, with an eye for details, managed the day-to-day business operations, while William spent his time working on the business's long-term operation and investments.

82   The Little Chateau de Blois on Fifth Avenue took three years and $3 million to build.

83   Idle Hour was the Vanderbilt's 800-acre summer country estate, a large, rambling, shingled villa overlooking the bay in Oakdale, on the south shore of Long Island.

Alva's desire for placing the Vanderbilt name at the top of society—even exceeding society potentates the Astors—was foremost in her mind. To this end she spent hundreds of thousands in hosting grand balls and special events. William became bored with all of this and absented himself on many occasions in favor of spending time with his beloved thoroughbreds, or living and traveling aboard his yacht. As his relationship with Alva became distant sometime after the birth of their youngest child, Harold, paying huge sums for Alva's building projects and society extravaganzas replaced his need to be with her, and was worth the price in his estimation. The marriage ended in 1895 amid charges of infidelity.

In 1903, William married the twice widowed[84] Anne Harriman Sands Rutherfurd in a very private ceremony in London. Her last husband had been Lewis Rutherfurd, brother of Winthrop Rutherfurd,[85] who had been seriously involved with William's daughter, Consuelo, a relationship that was broken up by her imperious mother, Alva.

Anne Harriman's father, Oliver, was a native of New York, where he had built a highly successful dry goods business. He later branched into investments and served on a number of corporate boards, including Bank of America and the Guaranty Trust Company. Anne inherited a modest fortune upon his death in 1904, and again later with the deaths of her two former husbands. William loved Anne and devoted himself to her happiness for the remaining seventeen years of his life.

The two siblings refilled their glasses as they shared the latest news from New York and their thoughts on disposing of their father's property. With the warmth of the gin infecting their senses, Harold decided to tell his brother about his plans to dispose of the remaining properties, hoping for agreement.

"Willie, I want you to know that I've put Idle Hour on the market. I've had some interest from a group that plans to convert it into a

---

84 Anne Harriman was first married to Samuel Stevens Sands, who died from the results of a hunting accident in 1892. She later married Lewis M. Rutherfurd, who died in 1899.

85 Winthrop Rutherfurd also maintained an Aiken home on Berrie Road.

country club, and I think we can get a fair price. And when I return to New York, I plan to sell Father's mansion at 660 Fifth Avenue as well, but I'm not sure about how well we'll do on price there. As you know, business development has crept up Fifth Avenue, and we have one of the very few remaining private residences there, floating in a sea of businesses. Father should have sold it years ago, but I know he kept it for Anne. Times have changed," said Harold with a sigh.

"Yes, you're right, Mike. Mother's chateau should have been sold years ago. And I only have bad memories of Idle Hour, with the fire[86] and all. Good riddance to them both," said Willie with a bravado aided by a gin glow.

At that moment Harold's facial expression radically changed to one of perplexed anxiety as he tilted his head and raised a finger to his lips. "Did you hear it, Willie?" he asked anxiously. He was now drawn to the open cottage window that faced the side yard. "There it is again! Willie, you must have heard it! I've been hearing it for the past week, but now it is considerably louder."

Willie stood behind and looked straight ahead over his brother's shoulder into the now darkened side yard. There was no moon on the night of March 16th to help them see, but they could follow the sound as it came from the direction of the blooming rose arch.

They heard a faint clink, clank of chain against iron repeating in cadence with the shuffling sound of slow, plodding footsteps, ever so quietly plodding in time with the growing volume of the clink, clank of chain. Then creaking wood was heard as old wooden steps being trod upon for the first time in many years, footsteps ascending.

"Willie, you must certainly hear it now?" pleaded Harold. "I've been hearing it every night this week, but never this loud."

"Yes, I do hear it now," whispered Willie as the two brothers' eyes searched the dark while they stood riveted before the side yard window.

---

86   In April 1899, newlyweds Willie and Virginia were honeymooning at the family's country estate when it caught fire in the early morning hours. All escaped unharmed, but the villa burned to the ground. It was subsequently rebuilt in stone.

Finally the rhythmic clink, clank of iron and chain stopped. And for a long moment an empty, deathly silence pervaded the yard until the piercing squeal of a rusty hinge being forced open to release its screeching voice after being shut up for many years broke the breezy air. This was immediately followed by the hollow clunk of heavy wood and the bass-pitched chord of a rope meeting quick resistance. Graveyard silence followed.

Neither brother uttered a word during these few moments, which seemed to last an eternity. They remained transfixed at the window.

The wind began to gain strength as it surged from the darkness, fluttering the curtains and flying full face into the brothers' stare. A now strong wind replaced the usual calm breeze that had carried the sweet scent of blooming roses during the past week, and now carried with it the foul odor of rotted remains. A sickening scent repulsive to the senses began to pervade the home. Harold slammed the window shut and turned white-faced to his brother.

"What in hell was that?" asked Willie.

"I don't know, but it started a couple of weeks ago and came each night at this same time, but without the odor. I could barely hear it then, but it kept getting louder, and tonight is the loudest yet," said Harold anxiously.

"Should we go out and check the yard?" asked Willie.

"No, let's just forget it. I'm ready to turn in anyway. And I would guess that you are too, after that long drive," said Harold.

March 17, 1921

A beautiful morning was developing in Aiken as the two brothers finished an early breakfast. It was the time of the morning when the sun had just broken the horizon and was beginning its climb. The early mist was quickly evaporating, and the glistening dew was giving off its last sparkle under the sun's growing intensity.

With the previous night's experience in mind, the two brothers went out to the side yard. As they walked past the green palmettos, white, pink, and red azaleas, and the newly budding oleanders, all appeared normal until at last they reached the rose arch. Both came to a dead stop as they saw that what once was an arch filled with beautiful red blooms only a day before was now a cluster of dead black, gray, and brown petals that hung among the now most prominent thorns. The entire arch from side to side and top to bottom was transformed from a beautiful natural arrangement of red to a sticky, black-hued rainbow of dead plant matter.

"Do you think this had anything to do with what we heard last night?" asked Willie.

"I don't know. But I don't think we should mention a word of this to Consuelo when she arrives today," said Harold.

"I agree," responded Willie.

The brothers lingered for a moment as they inspected the rose arch, looking for an explanation for their bizarre experience that they knew would never come. They started back to the house, having overlooked the metal object partially buried in the sand only a few feet from the rose arch—a rusted manacle attached to a black and rusted segment of chain.

THE REST OF THE STORY

William Kissam Vanderbilt

William K's happiest years of his life came with his second marriage to Anne Harriman Sands Rutherfurd in 1903. From that point on they split their time between William's chateau and their racing stable, Chateau St. Louis in Poissy, France, on their yacht, *Valiant*, and their homes in New York and Aiken. His love for racehorses was inherited from his father, a love he indulged at his Long Island and Aiken homes. Likewise, Anne was an avid horsewoman and was amicably accepted by William's children, who treated her with kindness, love, and respect.

William's first wife, Alva,[87] and mother of his children banned Anne and anyone who associated with her from any society gatherings over which she had control. She bore an intense hatred for Anne Harriman that she took to the grave in 1933.

William K. was seventy-one years old when he died on July 22, 1920. He had been attending horse races at Auteuil France on April 15th of that year when he suffered a heart attack. He remained at his Paris home until his death, after which his body was transported to New York, where he was interred in the family mausoleum on Staten Island. His estate at the time of his death was valued at approximately fifty-four million dollars. His heirs, financially unable to individually maintain the properties, liquidated them, including the Aiken winter retreat, Elm Court, some six years later.

Willie K. Vanderbilt Jr.

Like his father, Willie Jr. found happiness in a second marriage. In 1927, he married Rosamund Lancaster Warburton, former wife to an heir of the John Wanamaker department store fortune. Abandoning auto racing, he and Rosamund spent much of their time cruising the world, first aboard his yacht, *Ara*, and later, the *Alva*, so named after his mother. They became naturalists who collected marine and other species from around the world for display in his Centerport, Long Island home, Eagle's Nest,[88] where he established a museum wing for his collections.

---

87   Alva divorced William in March 1895, and married a Vanderbilt family friend, Oliver Hazard Perry Belmont, in January 1896. Belmont came from a prominent banking family and died suddenly in 1908.

88   Willie purchased the modest home in 1910, after separating from Virginia, as an alternative to the closely watched high society enclaves of Newport, Manhattan, and Palm Beach. He gradually added on to the home, creating several wings and a boat house. He used it and his Fisher Island home in Florida as launchpads for his oceanic ventures in the Caribbean and around the world.

Tragedy struck in 1933 when his twenty-six-year-old son, William III, was killed in an auto accident in South Carolina. William inherited his father's love of autos and speeding, and on a return trip to New York from his father's Fisher Island home in Florida, he struck a disabled vehicle parked on the roadside while traveling at a high rate of speed.

Eleven years after the death of his son, Willie Jr. died on January 8, 1944 at his New York home on Park Avenue, of a heart ailment. Out of his thirty-five-million-dollar estate, Rosamund inherited only five million. The rest went to satisfy federal and New York State taxes.

In just three years after Willie's death, Rosamund passed away at Eagle's Nest in 1947, as a result of breast cancer. She was fifty years of age.

Harold Sterling Vanderbilt

Throughout the 1930s, Harold involved himself in yacht racing and successfully defended America's Cup in 1930. He continued to participate in America's Cup, racing in 1934 and 1937, and served as commodore of the New York Yacht Club. He was involved in developing rules that would ultimately govern yacht racing in the future. He was posthumously elected to America's Cup Hall of Fame in 1993.

Harold remained with New York Central Railroad and was the only Vanderbilt actively involved in the company's management following Willie's death. By 1946, his stock was worth only one million dollars. The era of the Vanderbilt imperial dynasty was now over.

Harold spent much of his time at "Marble House," the Newport mansion built by his mother. In 1963, he joined with the Preservation Society of Newport to acquire the property and maintain it as a museum.

Harold died two days before his 86th birthday in 1970, and is buried in Portsmouth, Rhode Island.

Consuelo Vanderbilt Balsan

Beginning in her early childhood years, Consuelo's mother, Alva, took control over her every activity, grooming her to someday become a member of royalty. Her obsession found a successful end when she forced Consuelo to marry the philandering, penniless Duke of Marlborough. Her dowry to be paid to the duke's family was 2.5 million dollars, in addition to an annual stipend of $100,000 for life. She remained married to Marlborough for eleven unhappy years, and it wasn't until her second marriage to Frenchman Louis Jacques Balsan that she attained true happiness.

Perhaps because of the early treatment she received from her mother, Consuelo's demeanor was submissive and passive, but later in life she was to join with her mother in the cause of women's suffrage. As Vanderbilts they had influence in the cause, and occupied leadership roles within activist women's groups. Mother and daughter had reconciled after Consuelo's marriage to Balsan, and at the age of seventy-one, Alva sold property in New York and moved to France to be near her daughter. On January 26, 1933, Alva passed away, leaving the bulk of her now depleted estate to Consuelo.

Consuelo died on December 6, 1965, at the age of eighty-eight. At the time of her death, she left only $1 million from all of the millions she had received from her family.

The Vanderbilt home at 206 Colleton Avenue

William Vanderbilt bought the home in 1914. He died in 1920, and the home was sold by his heirs in 1926 to Mrs. Augustus Goodwin of Boston, Massachusetts. It was adapted for, and served in a number of different capacities in later years. In 1952, it was used as a restaurant and rooming house, primarily for workers constructing the Savannah River Site, the nuclear facility located south of Aiken. It was used as a clubhouse for the local Knights of Columbus group, and its last use was as a florist shop until it was destroyed by fire in January of 1978. For all of its multiple uses in later years following the death of William Vanderbilt, it was always known around Aiken as the "Old Courthouse." It was described as an historic Aiken landmark in news reports at the time of its total destruction by fire, with the only remaining evidence of its existence the wall surrounding the property and the plaque inlaid into the wall, "Elm Court."

Sources

Aiken Communications Inc., Aiken Standard, archives

Brewster, Lawrence Fay. *Summer Migrations and Resorts of South Carolina Lowcountry Planters*; 1970

Burgwyn, Diana. *Seventy-Five Years of the Curtis Institute of Music*; 1999

Gittelman, Steven H. *Willie K. Vanderbilt a Biography*; 2010

Gordon, Meryl. *Mrs. Astor Regrets: The Hidden Betrayals of a Family Beyond Reproach*; 2008

Graydon, Nell S. & Sizemore, Margaret D. *The Amazing Marriage of Marie Eustis & Josef Hofmann*; 1965

Historic Aiken Foundation. *A Splendid Time*; 2000

Kiernan, Frances. *The Last Mrs. Astor: A New York Story*; 2007

Kurin, Richard. *Hope Diamond*; 2007

L.A. Times.com, Archives, Cynthia Earle; 1985

Law, Donald M. *Forever Flourishing: The History of Aiken Preparatory School*; 1992

Lawrence, Kay. *Heroes, Horses & High Society: Aiken from 1540*; 1978

McLean, Evalyn Walsh. *Queen of Diamonds*; 2000

New York Times Corp., Archives

Peabody, Julian L. *Gran, A Personal Recollection*

Swanberg, W. A. *Whitney Father, Whitney Heiress*; 1980

Toole, G. L. *Ninety Years in Aiken County*; 1970

Vanderbilt, Arthur T., II. *Fortune's Children: The Fall of the House of Vanderbilt*; 1989

Wikimedia

Wikipedia, Free Encyclopedia

CPSIA information can be obtained at www.ICGtesting.com
Printed in the USA
LVOW102017051212

309924LV00006B/164/P

9 781432 797607